FELLOWSHIP OF THE STARS

Nine Science Fiction Stories

EDITED BY

TERRY CARR

with stories by
ALAN DEAN FOSTER
GEO. ALEC EFFINGER
FREDERIK POHL
MILDRED DOWNEY BROXON
FRITZ LEIBER
PAMELA SARGENT
ALAN BRENNERT
JOHN BRUNNER
URSULA K. LE GUIN

Simon and Schuster · New York

Library of Congress Cataloging in Publication Data

Carr, Terry, comp.
    Fellowship of the stars.

    CONTENTS: Carr, T. Introduction; Foster,
A. D. Dream done green; Effinger, G. A. Ashes
all my lust. [etc.]

    1. Science fiction, American.   I. Foster, Alan
Dean, 1946-   II. Title.
PZ1. C2339Fe   [PS648.S3]   813'.0876
74-12154
ISBN 0-671-21881-6

Contents

Introduction

Fellowship of the Stars is a compilation of all-new science fiction stories on the theme of friendship between human and alien beings. It's a theme with deep and fascinating significance.

For consider: Aren't we all, in reality, alien to each other? Each of us lives alone inside himself; we have no way of knowing whether, when we say "blue," the person to whom we're speaking perceives the same color we do; we can't be sure that any of the data given to us by our senses corresponds to that which other people receive. It may be that every human being who has ever lived has made his or her way in a world very different from the "reality" seen by other people.

We have languages by which we communicate, after a fashion; we make common agreements about what various words denote, and we assume that's all there is to it. But is it?

Explain "good" to me, or how "pain" feels to you. Describe precisely the smell of freshly cut grass.

Maybe you begin to see the difficulties . . . and we're talking now of people using the same language, living in the same country and in the same year. Do you suppose you could describe to a Tartar how liquid mercury feels? Do you think a citizen of Mohenjo-Daro could tell you what river water tastes like?

And if human beings experience these dramatic lapses in communication, what do you think might happen if we came into contact with beings who have lived their lives, and whose races have lived their histories, on worlds thousands of light-years from us?

The figure of the alien creature in science fiction can be seen as a dramatization of the person who stands next to us at any given moment: my wife, your classmate, someone else's co-worker. Because no matter how close together we may be spatially and temporally, in terms of perception we may be worlds apart.

Before science fiction developed as an art form, literature had a long tradition of the Outsider, the man who perceived things differently from most of us. He was the blind man who was a seer, the fool who knew no better than to speak the truth, the lunatic who saw realities none of the rest of us suspected.

He was, in modern scientific terms, the "control group," or the "reality tester." Only if his perceptions agreed with ours could we be sure that what we saw was true. And at that, his existence begged the question, because once we had agreed that his ideas had validity, the logical question became: How many Outsiders did it take to establish truth?

I see the figure of the science fiction alien as our contemporary version of the Outsider. Even if he's imaginary, he gives us data we wouldn't otherwise have; and if what he says strikes some chord within us, then maybe he's telling us something we should know, but don't . . . quite.

So this is a book about how reality seems to creatures who are vastly different from us, but whose perceptions are all the more valid because they aren't our own. And in each of these stories, once the alien has come onto the scene, the further question must be raised: How do we relate to him? If we become friends, what is the basis of our friendship? If we become enemies, why are our differences irreconcilable? And what do the answers tell us?

Science fiction is a literature of entertainment, but that doesn't mean it's "escape fiction." For after all, what can be more entertaining than the basic human process of learning about reality?

TERRY CARR

Oakland, California
March 1974

When one knows thee,
Then alien there is none,
Then no door is shut.
    —RABINDRANATH TAGORE

Dream Done Green

Alan Dean Foster

We live our daily lives surrounded by alien beings: dogs, cats, birds, all the nonhuman life forms of Earth. Our relationships with these creatures are limited, at present, to nonverbal, nonintellectual modes—but in the distant future, might not a method be found to raise the intelligence of animals? Here Alan Dean Foster tells a colorful and romantic story of the relationship between a human and a very intelligent horse . . . a horse who is a poet with a dream.

Alan Dean Foster is a comparatively new writer in science fiction, but already he's published half a dozen novels, among them The Tar-Aiym Krang *and* Icerigger.

The life of the woman Casperdan is documented in the finest detail, from birth to death, from head to toe, from likes to dislikes to indifferences.

Humans are like that.
The stallion Pericles we know only by his work.
Horses are like that.

We know it all began the year 1360 Imperial, 1822 After the Breakthrough, 2305 after the human Micah Schell found the hormone that broke the lock on rudimentary animal intelligence and enabled the higher mammals to attain at least the mental abilities of a human ten-year-old.

The quadrant was the Stone Crescent, the system Burr, the planet Calder, and the city Lalokindar.

Lalokindar was a wealthy city on a wealthy world. It ran away from the ocean in little bumps and curlicues. Behind it was virgin forest; in front, the Beach of Snow. The homes were magnificent and sat on spacious grounds, and that of the industrialist Dandavid was one of the most spacious and magnificent of all.

His daughter Casperdan was quite short, very brilliant, and by the standards of any age an extraordinary beauty. She had the looks and temperament of a Titania and the mind of a Baron Sachet. Tomorrow she came of legal age, which on Calder at that time was seventeen.

Under Calderian law she could then, as the oldest (and only) child, assume control of the family business or elect not to. Were one inclined to wager on the former course he would have found plenty of takers. It was only a formality. Girls of seventeen did not normally assume responsibility and control for multimillion credit industrial complexes.

Besides, following her birthday Casperdan was to be wed to Comore du Sable, who was handsome and intelligent (though not so rich as she).

Casperdan was dressed in a blue nothing and sat on the balustrade of the wide balcony overlooking Snow Beach and a bay of the Greengreen Sea. The old German shepherd trotted over to her, his claws clicking softly on the purple porphyry.

The dog was old and grayed and had been with the family for many years. He panted briefly, then spoke.

"Mistress, a strange mal is at the entrance."

Casperdan looked idly down at the dog.

"Who's its master?"

"He comes alone," the dog replied wonderingly.

"Well, tell him my father and mother are not at home and to come back tomorrow."

"Mistress"—the dog flattened his ears and lowered his head apologetically—"he says he comes to see *you*."

The girl laughed, and silver flute notes skittered off the polished stone floor.

"To see me? Stranger and stranger. And really alone?" She swung perfect legs off the balustrade. "What kind of mal is this?"

"A horse, mistress."

The flawless brow wrinkled. "Horse? Well, let's see this strange mal that travels alone."

They walked toward the foyer, past cages of force filled with rainbow colored tropical birds.

"Tell me, Patch . . . what is a 'horse'?"

"A large four-legged vegetarian." The dog's brow twisted with the pain of remembering. Patch was extremely bright for a dog. "There are none on Calder. I do not think there are any in the entire system."

"Offplanet, too?" Her curiosity was definitely piqued, now. "Why come to see me?"

"I do not know, mistress."

"And without even a human over h—"

Voice and feet stopped together.

The mal standing in the foyer was not as large as some.

La Moure's elephants were much bigger. But it was extraordinary in other ways. Particularly the head. Why . . . it was exquisite! Truly breathtaking. Not an anthropomorphic beauty, but something uniquely its own.

Patch slipped away quietly.

The horse was black as the Pit, with tiny exceptions. The right front forelock was silver, as was the diamond on its forehead. And there was a single streak of silver partway through the long mane, and another in the tail. Most mal wore only a lifepouch, and this one's was strapped to its neck. But it also wore an incongruous, utterly absurd hat of green felt, with a long feather protruding out and back.

With a start she realized she'd been staring . . . very undignified. She started toward it again. Now the head swung to watch her. She slowed and stopped involuntarily, somehow constrained from moving too close.

This is ridiculous! she thought. *It's only a mere mal, and not even very big. Why, it's even herbivorous!*

Then whence this strange fluttering deep in her tummy?

"You are Casperdan," said the horse suddenly. The voice was exceptional, too: a mellow tenor that tended to rise on concluding syllables, only to break and drop like a whitecap on the sea before the next word.

She started to stammer a reply, angrily composed herself.

"I am. I regret that I'm not familiar with your species, but I'll accept whatever the standard horse-man greeting is."

"I give no subservient greeting to any man," replied the horse. It shifted a hoof on the floor, which here was deep foam.

A *stranger and insolent to boot*, thought Casperdan furiously. She would call Patch and the household guards and . . . Her anger dissolved in confusion and uncertainty.

"How did you get past Row and Cuff?" Surely this harmless-looking, handless quadruped could not have overpowered the two lions. The horse smiled, showing white incisors.

"Cats, fortunately, are more subject to reason than many mal. And now I think I'll answer the rest of your questions.

"My name is Pericles. I come from Quaestor."

Quaestor! Magic, distant, Imperial capital! Her anger at this mal's insolence was subsumed in excitement.

"You mean you've actually traveled all the way from the capital . . . to meet me?"

"There is no need to repeat," the horse murmured, "only to confirm. It took a great deal of time and searching to find someone like you. I needed someone young . . . you are that. Only a young human would be responsive to what I have to offer. I needed someone bored, and you are wealthy as well as young."

"I'm not bored," Casperdan began defiantly, but he ignored her.

"I needed someone very rich, but without a multitude of ravenous relatives hanging about. Your father is a self-made tycoon, your mother an orphan. You have no relatives. And I needed someone with the intelligence and sensitivity to take orders from a mere mal."

This last was uttered with a disdain alien to Casperdan. Servants were not sarcastic.

"In sum," he concluded. "I need you."

"Indeed?" she mused, too overwhelmed by the outrageousness of this animal's words to compose a suitable rejoinder.

"Indeed," the horse echoed drily.

"And what, pray tell, do you need me for?"

The horse dropped its head and seemed to consider how best to continue. It looked oddly at her.

"Laugh now if you will. I have a dream that needs fulfilling."

"Do you, now? Really, this is becoming quite amusing."
What a story she'd have to tell at the preparty tomorrow!

"Yes, I do. Hopefully it will not take too many years."

She couldn't help blurting, "Years!"

"I cannot tell for certain. You see, I am a genius and a poet.
For me it's the dream part that's solid. The reality is what
lacks certitude. That's one reason why I need human help.
Need you."

This time she just stared at him.

"Tomorrow," continued the horse easily, "you will not
marry the man du Sable. Instead, you will sign the formal
Control Contract and assume directorship of the Dan family
business. You have the ability and brains to handle it. With
my assistance the firm will prosper beyond the wildest dreams
of your sire or any of the investors.

"In return, I will deed you a part of my dream, some of
my poetry, and something few humans have had for millennia.
I would not know of this last thing myself had I not chanced
across it in the Imperial archives."

She was silent for a brief moment, then spoke brightly.

"I have a few questions."

"Of course."

"First, I'd like to know if horses as a species are insane,
or if you are merely an isolated case."

He sighed, tossing his mane. "I didn't expect words to
convince you." The long black hair made sailor's knots with
sunbeams. "Do you know the Meadows of Blood?"

"Only by name." She was fascinated by the mention of the
forbidden place. "They're in the Ravaged Mountains. It's ru-
mored to be rather a pretty place. But no one goes there. The
winds above the canyon make it fatal to aircars."

"I have a car outside," the horse whispered. "The driver is
mal and knows of a winding route by which, from time to

time, it is possible to reach the Meadows. The winds war only above them. They are named, by the way, for the color of the flora there and not for a bit of human history . . . unusual.

"When the sun rises up in the mouth of a certain canyon and engulfs the crimson grasses and flowers in light . . . well, it's more than 'rather pretty.' "

"You've already been there," she said.

"Yes, I've already been." He took several steps and that powerful, strange face was close to hers. One eye, she noticed offhandedly, was red, the other blue.

"Come with me now to the Meadows of Blood and I'll give you that piece of dream, that something few have had for thousands of years. I'll bring you back tonight and you can give me your answer on the way.

"If it's 'no,' then I'll depart quietly and you'll never see me again."

Now, in addition to being both beautiful and intelligent, Casperdan also had her sire's recklessness.

"All right . . . I'll come."

When her parents returned home that night from the party and found their daughter gone, they were not distressed. After all, she was quite independent and, heavens, to be married tomorrow! When they learned from Patch that she'd gone off, not with a man, but with a strange mal, they were only mildly concerned. Casperdan was quite capable of taking care of herself. Had they known where she'd gone, things would have been different.

So nothing happened till the morrow.

"Good morning, Cas," said her father.

"Good morning, dear," her mother added. They were eating breakfast on the balcony. "Did you sleep well last night, and where did you go?"

The voice that answered was distant with other thoughts.

"I didn't sleep at all, and I went into the Ravaged Mountains. And there's no need to get excited, Father"—the old man sat back in his chair—"because as you see, I'm back safely and in one piece."

"But not unaffected," her mother stated, noticing the strangeness in her daughter's eyes.

"No, Mother, not unaffected. There will be no wedding." Before that lovely woman could reply, Casperdan turned to her father. "Dad, I want the Contract of Control. I intend to begin as director of the firm eight o'clock tomorrow morning. No, better make it noon . . . I'll need some sleep." She was smiling faintly. "And I don't think I'm going to get any right now."

On that she was right. Dandavid, that even-tempered but mercurial gentleman, got very, very excited. Between his bellows and her sobs, her mother leveled questions and then accusations at her.

When they found out about the incipient changeover, the investors immediately threatened to challenge it in court—law or no law, they weren't going to be guided by the decisions of an inexperienced snippet. In fact, of all those affected, the intended bridegroom took it best. After all, he was handsome and intelligent (if not as rich), and could damnwell find himself another spouse. He wished Casperdan well and consoled himself with his cello.

Her father (for her own good, of course) joined with the investors to challenge his daughter in the courts. He protested most strongly. The investors ranted and pounded their checkbooks.

But the judge was honest, the law machines incorruptible, and the precedents clear. Casperdan got her Contract and a year in which to prove herself.

Her first official action was to rename the firm Dream Enterprises. A strange name, many thought, for an industrial concern. But it was more distinctive than the old one. The investors grumbled, while the advertising men were delighted.

Then began a program of industrial expansion and acquisition unseen on somnolent Calder since the days of settlement. Dream Enterprises was suddenly everywhere and into everything. Mining, manufacturing, raw materials. These new divisions sprouted tentacles of their own and sucked in additional businesses.

Paper and plastics, electronics, nucleonics, hydrologics and parafoiling, insurance and banking, tridee stations and liquid tanking, entertainments and hydroponics and velosheeting.

Dream Enterprises became the wealthiest firm on Calder, then in the entire Stone Crescent.

The investors and Dandavid clipped their coupons and kept their mouths shut, even to ignoring Casperdan's odd relationship with an outsystem mal.

Eventually there came a morning when Pericles looked up from his huge lounge in the executive suite and stared across the room at Casperdan in a manner different from before.

The stallion had another line of silver in his mane. The girl had blossomed figuratively and figure-wise. Otherwise the years had left them externally unchanged.

"I've booked passage for us. Put Rollins in charge. He's a good man."

"Where are we going?" asked Casperdan. Not why, nor for how long, but where. She'd learned a great deal about the horse in the past few years.

"Quaestor."

Sudden sparkle in beautiful green eyes. "And then will you give me back what I once had?"

The horse smiled and nodded. "If everything goes smoothly."

In the Crescent, Dream Enterprises was powerful and respected and kowtowed to. In the Imperial sector it was different. There were companies on the capital planet that would classify it as a modest little family business. Bureaucratic tripwires here ran not for kilometers, but for light-years.

However, Pericles had threaded this maze many times before, and knew both men and mal who worked within the bowels of Imperial Government.

So it was that they eventually found themselves in the offices of Sim-sem Alround, Subminister for Unincorporated Imperial Territories.

Physically, Alround wasn't quite that. But he did have a comfortable bureaucratic belly, a rectangular face framed by long bushy sideburns and curly red hair tinged with white. He wore the current fashion, a monocle. For all that, and his dry occupation, he proved charming and affable.

A small stream ran through his office, filled with trout and tadpoles and cattails. Casperdan reclined on a long couch made to resemble solid granite. Pericles preferred to stand.

"You want to buy some land, then?" queried Alround after drinks and pleasantries had been exchanged.

"My associate will give you the details," Casperdan informed him. Alround shifted his attention from human to horse without a pause. Naturally he'd assumed . . .

"Yes sir?"

"We wish to purchase a planet," said Pericles. "A small planet . . . not very important."

Alround waited. Visitors interested in small transactions didn't get in to see the Subminister himself.

"Just one?"

"One will be quite sufficient."

Alround depressed a switch on his desk. A red light flashed on, indicated that all details of the conversation to follow were now being taken down for the Imperial records.

"Purpose of purchase?"

"Development."

"Name of world?"

"Earth."

"All right . . . fine," said the Subminister. Abruptly, he looked confused. Then he smiled. "Many planets are called Earth by their inhabitants or discoverers. Which particular Earth is this?"

"*The* Earth. Birthplace of mankind and malkind. Old Earth. Also known variously as Terra and Sol III."

The Subminister shook his head. "Never heard of it."

"It is available, though?"

"We'll know in a second." Alround studied the screen in his desk.

Actually it took several minutes before the gargantuan complex of metal and plastic and liquid buried deep in the soil beneath them could come up with a reply.

"Here it is, finally," said Alround. "Yes, it's available . . . by default, it seems. The price will be . . ." He named a figure which seemed astronomical to Casperdan and insanely low to the horse.

"Excellent!" husked Pericles. "Let us conclude the formalities now."

"Per'," Casperdan began, looking at him uncertainly. "I don't know if we have enough . . ."

"Some liquidation will surely be necessary, Casperdan, but we will manage."

The Subminister interrupted.

"Excuse me . . . there's something you should know before we go any further. I *can* sell you Old Earth, but there is an attendant difficulty."

"Problems can be solved, difficulties overcome, obstructions removed," said the horse irritably. "Please get on with it."

Alround sighed. "As you wish." He drummed the required buttons. "But you'll need more than your determination to get around this one.

"You see, it seems no one knows how to get to Old Earth anymore . . . or even where it is."

Later, strolling among the teeming mobs of Imperial City, Casperdan ventured a hesitant opinion.

"I take it this means it's not time for me to receive my part of the dream again?"

"Sadly, no, my friend."

Her tone turned sharp. "Well, what do you intend to do now? We've just paid quite an enormous number of credits for a world located in obscurity, around the corner from no-place."

"We shall return to Calder," said the horse with finality, "and continue to expand and develop the company." He pulled back thick lips in an equine smile.

"In all the research I did, in all my careful planning and preparation, never once did I consider that the location of the home world might have been lost.

"So now we must go back and hire researchers to research, historians to historize, and ships to search and scour the skies in sanguine directions. And wait."

A year passed, and another, and then they came in small multiples. Dream Enterprises burgeoned and grew, grew and thrived. It moved out of the Stone Crescent and extended its influence into other quadrants. It went into power generation and multiple metallurgy, into core mining and high fashion.

And finally, of necessity, into interstellar shipping.

There came the day when the captain with the stripped-down scoutship was presented to Casperdan and the horse

Pericles in their executive office on the two hundred and twentieth floor of the Dream building.

Despite a long, long, lonely journey the captain was alert and smiling. Smiling because the endless trips of dull searching were over. Smiling because he knew the company reward for whoever found a certain aged planet.

Yes, he'd found Old Earth. Yes, it was a long way off, and in a direction only recently suspected. Not in toward the galactic center, but out on the Arm. And yes, he could take them there right away.

The shuttleboat settled down into the atmosphere of the planet. In the distance, a small yellow sun burned smooth and even.

Pericles stood at the observation port of the shuttle as it drifted planetward. He wore a special protective suit, as did Casperdan. She spared a glance at the disconsolate mal. Then she did something she did very rarely. She patted his neck.

"You musn't be too disappointed if it's not what you expected, Per'." She was trying to be comforting. "History and reality have a way of not coinciding."

It was quiet for a long time. Then the magnificent head, lowered now, turned to face her. Pericles snorted bleakly.

"My dear, dear Casperdan, I can speak eighteen languages fluently and get by in several more, and there are no words in any of them for what I feel. 'Disappointment'? Consider a nova and call it warm. Regard Quaestor and label it well-off. Then look at me and call me disappointed."

"Perhaps," she continued, not knowing what else to say, "it will be better on the surface."

It was worse.

They came down in the midst of what the captain called a mild local storm. To Casperdan it was a neat slice of the mythical hell.

Stale yellow-brown air whipped and sliced its way over high dunes of dark sand. The uncaring mounds marched in endless waves to the shoreline. A dirty, dead beach melted into brackish water and a noisome green scum covered it as far as the eye could see. A few low scrubs and hearty weeds eked out a perilous existence among the marching dunes, needing only a chance change in the wind to be entombed alive.

In the distance, stark, bare mountains gave promise only of a higher desolation.

Pericles watched the stagnant sea for a long time. Over the intercom his voice was shrunken, the husk of a whisper, those compelling tones beaten down by the moaning wind.

"Is it like this everywhere, Captain?"

The spacer replied unemotionally. "Mostly. I've seen far worse worlds, sir . . . but this one is sure no prize. If I may be permitted an opinion, I'm damned if I can figure out why you want it."

"Can't you feel it, Captain?"

"Sir?" The spacer's expression under his faceglass was puzzled.

"No, no, I guess you cannot. But I do, Captain. Even though this is not the Earth I believed in, I still feel it. I fell in love with a dream. The dream seems to have departed long ago, but the memory of it is still here, still here . . ." Another long pause, then, "You said 'mostly'?"

"Well, yes." The spacer turned and gestured at the distant range. "Being the discovering vessel, we ran a pretty thorough survey, according to the general directives. There are places— near the poles, in the higher elevations, out in the middle of the three great oceans—where a certain amount of native life still survives. The cycle of life here has been shattered, but a few of the pieces are still around.

"But mostly, it's like this." He kicked at the sterile sand.

"Hot or cold desert—take your pick. The soil's barren and infertile, the air unfit for man or mal.

"We did find some ruins . . . God, they were old! You saw the artifacts we brought back. But except for its historical value, this world strikes me as particularly worthless."

He threw another kick at the sand, sending flying shards of mica and feldspar and quartz to the highways of the wind.

Pericles had been thinking. "We won't spend much more time here, Captain." The proud head lifted for a last look at the dead ocean. "There's not much to see."

They'd been back in the offices on Calder only a half-month when Pericles announced his decision.

Dream-partner or no dream-partner, Casperdan exploded.

"You quadrupedal cretin! Warm-blooded sack of fatuous platitudes! Terraforming is only a theory, a hypothesis in the minds of sick romantics. It's impossible!"

"No one has ever attempted it," countered the horse, un-ruffled by her outburst.

"But . . . my God!" Casperdan ran delicate fingers through her flowing blonde hair. "There are no facilities for doing such a thing . . . no company, no special firms to consult. Why, half the industries that would be needed for such a task don't even exist."

"They will," Pericles declared.

"Oh yes? And just *where* will they spring from?"

"You and I are going to create them."

She pleaded with him. "Have you gone absolutely mad? We're not in the miracle business, you know."

The horse walked to the window and stared down at the Greengreen Sea. His reply was distant. "No . . . we're in the dream business . . . remember?"

A cloud of remembrance came over Casperdan's exquisite

face. For a moment, she did—but it wasn't enough to stem the tide of objection. Though she stopped shouting.

"Please, Per' . . . take a long, logical look at this before you commit yourself to something that can only hurt you worse in the end."

He turned and stared evenly at her. "Casperdan, for many, many years now I've done nothing but observe things with a reasoned eye, done nothing without thinking it through beginning, middle, and end and all possible ramifications, done nothing I wasn't absolutely sure of completing.

"Now I'm going to take a chance. Not because I want to do it this way, but because I've run out of options. I'm not mad, no . . . but I *am* obsessed." He looked away from her.

"But I can't do it without you, damn it, and you know why . . . no mal can head a private concern that employs humans."

She threw up her hands and stalked back to her desk. It was silent in the office for many minutes. Then she spoke softly.

"Pericles, I don't share your obsession . . . I've matured, you know . . . now I think I can survive with just the memory of my dream-share. But you rescued me from my own narcissism. And you've given me . . . other things. If you can't shake this psychotic notion of yours, I'll stay around till you can."

Horses and geniuses don't cry . . . ah, but poets . . . !

And that is how the irony came about—that the first world where terraforming was attempted was not some sterile alien globe, but Old Earth itself. Or as the horse Pericles is reputed to have said, "Remade in its own image."

The oceans were cleared . . . the laborious, incredibly costly first step. That done, and with a little help from two thousand chemists and bioengineers, the atmosphere began to cleanse itself. That first new air was neither sweet nor fresh—but neither was it toxic.

Grasses are the shock troops of nature. Moved in first, the special tough strains took hold in the raped soil. Bacteria and nutrients were added, fast-multiplying strains that spread rapidly. From the beachheads near the arctic and in the high mountains flora and fauna were reintroduced.

Then came the major reseeding of the superfast trees: spruce and white pine, juniper and birch, cypress and mori and teak, fir and ash. And from a tiny museum on Duntroon, long preserved Sequoia and citrus.

Eventually there was a day when the first flowers were replanted. The hand-planting of the first bush—a green rose—was watched by the heads of the agricultural staffs, a black horse, and a ravishing young woman in the postbloom of her first rejuvenation.

That's when Pericles registered the Articles. They aroused only minor interest within the sleepy, vast Empire. The subject was good for a few days' conversation before the multitudes returned to more important news.

But among the mal, there was something in the Articles and accompanying pictures that tugged at nerves long dormant, nerves buried deep and forgotten, nerves long since sealed off in men and mankind by time and by choice. Something that pulled each rough soul toward an unspectacular planet circling an unremarkable star in a distant corner of space.

So the mal went back to Old Earth. Not all, but many. They left the trappings of Imperial civilization and confusing intelligence and went to the first mal planet.

More simply, they went home.

There they labored not for man, but for themselves. And when a few interested humans applied for permission to emigrate there, they were turned back by the private patrol. For the Articles composed by the horse Pericles forbade the introduction of man to Old Earth. Those articles were written in endurasteel, framed in paragraphs of molten duralloy. Neither human curiosity nor money could make a chip in them.

It was clear to judges and law machines that while the Articles (especially the phrase about "the meek finally inheriting the Earth") might not have been good manners or good taste, they were very good law.

It was finished.

It was secured.

It was given unto the mal till the end of time.

Casperdan and Pericles left the maze that was now Dream Enterprises and went to Old Earth. They came to stand on the same place where they'd stood decades before.

Now clean low surf grumbled and subsided on a beach of polished sand that was home to shellfish and worms and brittle stars. They stood on a field of low, waving green grass. In the distance a family of giraffe moved like sentient signal towers toward the horizon. The male saw them, swung its long neck in greeting. Pericles responded with a long, high whinny.

To their left, in the distance, the first mountains began. Not bare and empty now, but covered with a mat of thick evergreen crowned with new snow.

They breathed in the heady scent of fresh clover and distant honeysuckle.

"It's done," he said.

Casperdan nodded and began to remove her clothes. Someday she would bring a husband down here. She was the sole exception in the Articles. Her golden hair fell in waves to her waist. Someday, yes . . . but for now . . .

"You know, Pericles, it really wasn't necessary. All this, I mean."

The stallion pawed at the thick loam underfoot.

"What percentage of dreams are necessary, Casperdan? You know, for many mal intelligence was not a gift but a curse. It was always that way for man, too, but he had more time to grow into it. For the mal it came like lightning, as a shock. The mal are still tied to their past—to this world. As I am still tied. Have you ever seen mal as happy as they are here?

"Certainly sentience came too quickly for the horse. According to the ancient texts we once had a special relationship with man that rivaled the dog's. That vanished millennia ago. The dog kept it, though, and so did the cat, and certain others. Other mal never missed it because they never had it. But the horse did, and couldn't cope with the knowledge of that loss that intelligence brought. There weren't many of us left, Casperdan.

"But we'll do well here. This is home. Man would feel it too, if he came here now. Feel it . . . and ruin this world all over again. That's why I wrote the Articles."

She was clad only in shorts now and to her great surprise found she was trembling slightly. She hadn't done that since she was fifteen. How long ago was that? Good God, had she ever been fifteen? But her face and figure were those of a girl of twenty. Rejuvenation.

"Pericles, I want back what you promised. I want back what I had in the Meadows of Blood in the Ravaged Mountains."

"Of course," he replied, as though it had happened yesterday. A mal's sense of time is different from man's, and Pericles' was different from that of most mal.

"You know, I have a confession to make." She was startled to see that the relentless dreamer was embarrassed!

"It was done only to bribe you, you know. But in truth . . . in truth, I think I enjoyed it as much as you. And I'm ashamed, because I still don't understand *why*."

He kicked at the dirt.

She smiled understandingly. "It's the old bonds you talk about, Per'. I think they must work both ways."

She walked up to him and entwined her left hand in his mane, threw the other over his back. A pull and she was up. Her movement was done smoothly . . . she'd practiced it ten thousand times in her mind.

Both hands dug tightly into the silver-black mane. Leaning forward, she pressed her cheek against the cool neck and felt ropes of muscle taut beneath the skin. The anticipation was so painful it hurt to speak.

"I'm ready," she whispered breathlessly.

"So am I," he replied.

Then the horse Pericles gave her what few humans had had for millennia, what had been outlawed in the Declaration of Animal's Rights, what they'd shared in the Meadows of Blood a billion years ago.

Gave her back the small part of the dream that was hers.

Tail flying, hooves digging dirt, magnificent body moving effortlessly over the rolling hills and grass, the horse became brother to the wind as he and his rider thundered off toward the waiting mountains . . .

And that's why there's confusion in the old records. Because they knew all about Casperdan in the finest detail, but all they knew about the horse Pericles was that he was a genius and a poet. Now, there's ample evidence as to his genius. But the inquisitive are puzzled when they search and find no record of his poetry.

Even if they knew, they wouldn't understand.

The poetry, you see, was when he moved.

Ashes All My Lust

Geo. Alec Effinger

*When Earthmen explore the planets of other star
systems they'll almost certainly come into contact
with other intelligent races—creatures who may have
talents that we don't, and won't, suspect. Geo. Alec
Effinger imagines a species of aliens who can repay
Earthmen for friendship by providing them with
more pleasure than the humans may want.*

*Geo. Alec Effinger is recognized as one of the best
writing talents to enter the field in recent years. His
novels include* What Entropy Means to Me *and*
Relatives.

Tobblen stopped and looked toward the small stand of
trees. It was about a half-mile away, across the silent gray
plain. There were no more than a couple of hundred trees in

all, but until recently that copse had been his whole universe. For fifteen years he had lived among the trees, peeking out only occasionally for a look at the prairie, to see the scattered islands of scrub growth, or the distant streaks of black that might either be huge beasts or mere shadows of passing clouds.

A small tribe of humans lived within the grove, sheltered there from the observation of predators. The sparse vegetation of the plain fed the bottom links of the vertebrate food chain; in the generations since their ancestors had been stranded on the world, the humans had had to change their way of life to maintain their place at its top. It would be horribly easy to slip from the rank of premier hunter down to the level of common prey. Children, being especially vulnerable, were kept close to home. They were guarded and educated by the community, which, for defensive and practical reasons, was necessarily located permanently within the copse. The primary source of food was the tribe's hunters; however, the tribe was too weak to pursue the nomadic existence which that kind of lifestyle implied.

Tobblen was sixteen years old. He was now an adult, permitted and expected to find the necessities of life out on the plain, which for so long had been prohibited to him. He had his own weapons, with which he was still inexpert. He had built a shelter beneath a sprawling micha tree for himself and Darkai, his young wife. All the trappings of maturity had suddenly been thrust on him; nevertheless, his childhood fears had not entirely been left behind. No, rather, they had been strengthened by the insecurity of his new independence. The fight for life on this world was unfairly rigged against the humans. The beasts of the plain matured in a matter of months; the humans' babies required care for years, threatening the safety of the entire tribe. The only solution was to force the young ones out on their own as soon as possible. If the weaker individuals suffered in the transition, it either strengthened them or destroyed them. The ones who couldn't adjust fell to the claws, fangs, or stings of the predators. This was the best thing for the tribe.

The route back to the copse was clear. Tobblen couldn't see any islands of spiky blue grass along the way he'd chosen. He was familiar with the two abandoned wasp holes, about a third of the way to the settlement. The wasp holes, crumbling now with disuse, were still places to avoid. Tobblen had never seen one of the giant wasps close up, but he had seen hunters who lucklessly or carelessly allowed themselves to be attacked by them. The men were carried back from the plain by their companions; the victims quivered horribly in the strange paralysis of the wasps' poison sting. Those doomed men were set to rest beneath the huge death tree in the center of the grove, and attended by their wives and relations. Their faces stretched more terribly as the hours passed, their breathing became ragged, their muscles cramped and contorted their bodies into grotesque postures. Then, always, they died.

Far to his right Tobblen saw Igari, an old man who had hunted with Tobblen on the youth's first forage. "Hoa!" shouted Tobblen, waving his arm, but Igari did not notice. To Tobblen's left was Shomler, Darkai's brother. The three men worked their way slowly, watchfully, back toward the stand of trees. Tobblen stared at the ground ahead of him, trusting that the line of hunters at his back would warn him of danger from that quarter. Small shrews and mice jumped out of his line of march as he approached, scurrying away among the clumps of dry, gray weeds. Nothing larger was evident and, though it meant there would be no food, Tobblen was glad. It also meant no danger.

"We're going to look pretty stupid when we get back," called Shomler.

"I don't worry about that," said Tobblen. "Today we'll

look stupid. Tomorrow we'll look *hungry*."

Shomler laughed, a coarse, raucous noise that always annoyed Tobblen. "We can bloody your head," said Shomler. "Before the others see us, we can pound you with stones. Then we can make up a great story about a grass cat or something. You can be a hero. If we bloody you enough, I can be a hero, too."

"I don't ever want to be a hero," said Tobblen slowly. "Darkai doesn't want that, either. She just wants me home." The men marched on toward the grove for a few paces. Then Tobblen spoke up again. "Yes," he said, "and if you think you can lay a rock alongside my head, you can just try it. You'll end up a bigger hero than you ever counted on." Shomler laughed, but said nothing.

The weapons of the humans were primitive: long sticks with points of bone, others with the stings of slaughtered wasps, all tipped with the wasps' own poison. It wasn't that the humans knew no better, but that they could do no better. Forced into a defensive attitude, they accepted both poverty and gradual cultural deterioration. Generations ago, when the original party had been stranded on the planet, great armies of wasps had caused the humans to flee in helpless panic. Now their descendants, scattered across the face of the world, separated by unmapped miles of the unvaried gray plain, clung to whatever of their old knowledge was practical, and regretfully put aside the luxury of civilization.

But though they retained the manner of their fathers, and not the details, they lived united by one aim: to eradicate the race of wasps that had made the humans slaves to weakness and fear.

Tobblen took a detour around the first of the old wasp holes. Unlike the city-building wasps, which constructed huge camplike settlements on the plains, the wasps that had dug these holes were members of a rarer variety. The hole dwellers were less social; they did not seem to share the instinctive needs for cooperation and industry that possessed the city builders. The digger wasps were smaller than the social insects, but quicker to anger and more deadly in battle. Their poison was considerably more concentrated, and therefore highly prized by the humans.

"First nest," called Tobblen.

"Right," answered Igari.

"Careful, now," said Shomler.

Tobblen paused a few feet from the old wasp hole. Igari closed in from the right, and Shomler from the left. Meanwhile, Tobblen checked behind; the second line of hunters had nearly caught up. Tobblen bent down and picked up a large rock. He raised his spear with his right hand and threw the stone into the wasp hole with his left. Igari and Shomler crouched, ready to attack. Nothing happened. There was no sound but the wind rustling the tall spike grass around the hole. There was no motion but the languid waving of the weeds. Tobblen let out a deep breath and lowered his spear. He waved to the others to continue.

"Let's get home," he said.

"Naw," said Shomler, laughing loudly. "You only take point position once every two weeks. You ought to get as much fun out of it as you can."

"Fun!" said Tobblen disgustedly. "Shomler, someday you're going to come out here all brave and puffed out, and you're going to stumble on a rock. Before you hit the ground, one of those blue spike weeds is going to stab you right through your heart. We'll have to carry you back, and when that sexy Naelly of yours starts bawling, we'll tell her how you died. Some hero! She won't stop laughing for a month!" Shomler's grin disappeared. He stopped and stared angrily at his brother-in-law, who only laughed. "Come on, Shomler," he said, "or we'll leave you behind!" The other refused to answer. Tobblen shook his head and walked on.

He had covered about half the distance to the second wasp hole when he was startled by a shout from his right. He turned, ready to attack; he saw Igari, kneeling in the dry gray sod, one arm across his face. Blood trickled down his forearm and fell to the grass. Beyond the older man Tobblen saw Shomler, running farther away, carrying his spear aloft and another at his side. Evidently Shomler had struck Igari and taken the man's spear. Tobblen was bewildered; he beckoned one of the men in the second line to tend to Igari, and waved at the rest to follow after Shomler.

The other youth was racing straight toward an island of blue spike grass, one of the hillocks Tobblen was carefully avoiding. Before Shomler reached the island, though, he turned to gauge his pursuers. "Hurry up, Tobblen, you bastard!" he screamed. He waved his arms wildly. Tobblen was running as fast as he could, leading the other hunters. A few seconds before Tobblen caught up to his brother-in-law, Shomler turned and ran away. "Here," cried Shomler. "Come on, hero. You idiot!" And he launched his spear with all the strength of his huge body into the middle of the island of spike grass.

"Hold it!" yelled Tobblen, but it was too late. From ten yards away, the angry sound of the wasp's giant wings was plainly audible. The vicious insect rose up above the weeds and seemed to hover, staring at Shomler. The wasp was uninjured by the first spear, but it wasn't in any mood for charity. It climbed a little more, then plunged toward Shomler. The youth waited the space of a heartbeat while the wasp fell into pointblank range. He didn't throw the second spear; he grasped it with both hands near the end of the haft, and drove it into the wasp's body, using the insect's momentum to drive the point deep.

The impact knocked Shomler to his knees. "See," he cried, "that's the way!" The spear was torn from his hands as the huge wasp crashed to the ground. Shomler bent to pick up a rock to smash the wasp's head. Tobblen recovered his senses and ran to Shomler's aid. Before he could get close enough, the wasp had wriggled and rolled nearer to Shomler. The youth raised his rock, but before he could bring it down to end the life of the thing, it curled its body and stabbed upward, catching Shomler in the thigh with its sting. Shomler screamed shrilly and clutched his leg. The wasp's sting was imbedded deeply; as the insect thrashed in its agonies, it threw Shomler to the ground. The air was filled with the inhuman noises of the wasp and the dreadful cries of Shomler. Tobblen stood above the wasp and thrust the point of his spear into its head, just behind one of the great, faceted eyes.

For a few seconds Tobblen could not speak. He stared at the lifeless wasp, a feeling of revulsion and weariness filling him. Shomler had stopped screaming. As the wasp's poison traveled through his body, his anguish would increase. He made strange, awful mewling sounds now. Tobblen pointed to two of the other hunters; they went to Shomler and picked him up. It would be a quiet, sorrowful march home. The two men carrying Shomler led the way, followed by the man who supported the still-dazed Igari. Then came the rest of the party, dragging the dead insect. Tobblen fell behind, looking for the spear Shomler had thrown into the hillock. Even at times like these, there were rules of survival that couldn't be overlooked.

When they reached the encampment within the trees, the men of the hunting party needed no orders from Tobblen. The women who had gathered at the edge of the grove, their eyes straining to catch a first glimpse of the returning men, set up a low wailing when they recognized that it was Shomler being carried back, not a supply of meat. The weary hunters proceeded straight to the death tree, except for Tobblen, who had the duty of informing Naelly, Shomler's wife.

The shelter which Shomler had built for his wife and infant daughter was like most, a mere lean-to with heavy branches for framework and tangled evergreen boughs for roof and sides. Naelly was boiling water to make a porridge for her husband's supper. Tobblen stood watching for a few seconds. Finally, the young woman noticed him and looked up curiously.

"You heard the women over there?" he asked.

Naelly nodded. She was a very beautiful woman, not yet seventeen years old. Her delicate face was streaked with dirt, and her long black hair was matted with leaves and twigs, but there was a strength and a dignity to her manner that overcame the difficulties of her life. "I guess you didn't get any food again," she said, smiling sadly.

"Ayah," said Tobblen. He felt sick; he wanted to get the matter over with, but the quickest way was also the most brutal. "We had some trouble out there. Somebody got stung by a wasp. Shomler." After he got the words out, Tobblen felt worse. He stood above the girl and watched her. The chorus of shrieking from the area of the death tree convinced Naelly that Tobblen wasn't playing some cruel joke. Her expression changed from disbelief to shock to utter horror. She began to cry loudly; Tobblen muttered a few words and slipped uncomfortably away. He still had to tell his wife, Shomler's sister, the same story.

When Tobblen arrived at his own rugged shelter, his wife was gone. A small stone of water had been left to boil; evidently Darkai had heard the mourning and gone to investigate. Tobblen sighed. He was glad that it wouldn't be necessary to break the news to her, too. He removed the water from the fire and started toward the death tree to meet her.

Already the day had deepened into dusk. The shadows of the trees quickened in the light from dozens of cooking fires. In the gloom Tobblen saw his wife walking slowly toward him. There was still a large group of people around the death tree; Darkai, however, had seen enough, and was staggering back to the shelter. Tobblen put his arm around her. He was shocked when she shrugged it off. She ran on ahead, sobbing. He let her go. He didn't know what else to do.

He followed hesitantly. When he arrived at the shelter, his porridge supper was nearly cooked. He touched Darkai's shoulder, but she only sobbed and turned away.

"I'm sorry about your brother," he said.

She stared at him for a moment. "No, you're not," she said hoarsely. "You're *glad*. He was always better than you. He was a better hunter. Everybody knew it. And you want Naelly." Tobblen stood silently, his mouth open to reply. He couldn't think of anything to say. "It was your fault," said Darkai bitterly. "You were the leader. You let him die."

"Did anyone tell you how it happened?" asked Tobblen.

"Ah, they want to protect you. Shomler will die, sure enough. He won't be able to tell the truth."

"Do you really believe that?"

Darkai nodded, then began crying loudly again. At last she sank slowly to the soft floor of the grove, weeping and pounding the moist ground with her fists. Tobblen took a bowl of porridge and retired into the shelter. A long while later Darkai joined him. She sat down quietly and put her head on his arm.

"It wasn't true, what I said," she said. "I mean, I didn't really believe all that. You do want Naelly, though, don't you?"

Tobblen wiped the tears on her cheeks with his grimy fist. He smiled, although he didn't feel so happy inside. "Sure," he said, "we all do. That's what we talk about out on the plain. That's why . . ." He let his voice trail off when he realized what he was about to say. Darkai finished his thought in her mind, however, and once more began to cry. Tobblen put his arm around her shoulders and held her. In a while it was completely dark in the shelter; shortly after that she fell asleep, and Tobblen sat in the black stillness, thinking.

The next day, just as the sun edged above the plain's horizon, Tobblen joined the group of hunters. They had assembled by the death tree, beneath which Shomler had spent the night. Tobblen's brother-in-law had died several hours earlier, and everyone in the small community had known the exact minute. Shomler's anguished screams had grown softer during the night; then, as his voice became hoarse and inhuman, they stopped suddenly. It had been a relief for Tobblen at last, but he had not slept even after that. Now the hunters, grieving but still bound by the harsh duties of their life, came together around Shomler's stiff, awful corpse. The leader for the day's hunt was Hanest, a young man a year or two older than Tobblen. Hanest stared at his dead friend for a few moments, then turned and slowly looked at Tobblen. "Come on," said Hanest at last. "By the time we get back, the women will have buried him. We have to think about other things." The men walked away from the death tree, their heads bowed and their expressions thoughtful. They took up the regular hunt formation; Tobblen, having just served as point leader, was due for rotation back to one of the third line flanks, a position of responsibility only slightly less than leader. Hanest stopped him at the edge of the grove. "Look," he said, "why don't you take up a slot in second line? You had a hard day yesterday. I'll get Pura to trade with you."

Tobblen frowned. "That's all right," he said. "I'm fine. I don't need any kind of special treatment."

Hanest spoke again, but this time his voice was hard, full of his temporary authority, something the daily point leader rarely needed to display. "Take second line right," he said. He turned away, ending the discussion, and called to the other man. "Pura, I want you to take Tobblen's place in third line today." Pura nodded silently and stared for a moment at Tobblen. They all formed up and moved slowly into the stiff gray scrub.

There were many potential dangers on the plain—grass cats, the letmoths that drained a grown man of blood in seconds, small venomous plants that could be easily overlooked among the constant, drab colors of the prairie—but the hunters went out with one special fear articulated in their minds: the wasps. The giant insects had formed a part of every person's life since earliest childhood; hunters had returned from the plain stung and paralyzed, like Shomler, and the little children had watched in horror and innocent curiosity from the safety of their mothers' sides. Stories about children taken away for their misdeeds by flying wasps were common enough, but these tales always disappeared for a few weeks after the death of one of the hunters. They reappeared sooner or later, though, reinforced by the first-hand evidence of a man in utter agony.

The human community in the small wooded area could not afford the luxury of scientific experimentation or geographic discovery. They had neither the time nor the personnel to spare. Therefore, Tobblen's people were unsure about the exact number of different varieties of wasp that inhabited their immediate area of the plain. They knew of the slow, giant wasp, the sort that had defended itself against Shomler's unwise attack; they knew of the even huger variety, that lived in social groups and built moundlike cities of immense size. A far-ranging hunting party had once come across an abandoned wasp city several miles from the human settlement, and did not know how to explain it until one man found a long, crumbling tunnel filled with the remains of larval cells. There were probably other varieties, but the humans didn't especially care to catalog them. To the men on the hunting parties, and to their anxious wives and children, they were all wasps and they were all hated.

Tobblen marched quietly across the plain, holding his spear ready but letting his mind wander. In the second line, there was not much chance that he'd be surprised by any danger. He was protected by a line of men in front of him and another behind him; he did not like the idea that Hanest had stationed him in second line because of Tobblen's actions the day before. It seemed to Tobblen that Hanest, like Darkai and perhaps the rest of the community, blamed Shomler's death on Tobblen's lack of maturity. It didn't seem fair.

Suddenly, the youth's thoughts were interrupted by a shout from behind. "Get it!" somebody yelled. Tobblen turned and saw Pura, the older man taking Tobblen's position in the rear line, running across the plain. Behind Pura followed the rest of the third line. Tobblen couldn't see what kind of animal had been flushed; he waited for Hanest's instructions.

"It's a wasp," shouted Gattol, next to Tobblen.

"I don't see it," said Tobblen.

"It's small. There, Pura has it!" While the other hunters watched, Pura swung his spear and struck the insect, which was trying to escape but flew close to the ground. Tobblen supposed that Pura had injured the wasp earlier, when he first found it. He hit it again now, and the insect dropped to the ground. Pura raised his spear.

"Careful, now," shouted Tobblen. "Watch out for the sting. That's just how Shomler—"

"He can handle it, all right," said Gattol. "He doesn't have some stupid kid getting in his way." Tobblen stared at the other man, but said nothing. Pura brought his spear down and pinned the wasp to the ground. The other hunters from the third line helped kill the insect, and began to strip it of its valuable parts.

Tobblen leaned on the haft of his spear and watched the men. The wasp was less than half the size of the insect that had killed Shomler, another variety perhaps. It did not take long for Pura and his companions to finish stripping the dead wasp. "All right," called Hanest, "let's go on. Pura, you can handle all that stuff by yourself, can't you? Well, trade places with Gattol in the second line. We can't go back with just that, and you'll be a liability in third line carrying it all. Is that all right with you, Gattol?" The man next to Tobblen just nodded and took up his new position. They moved out again.

Tobblen felt peculiarly alone, as they walked toward a distant island of blue spike grass on the horizon. It seemed to him that all the others had made an unspoken agreement to ignore Tobblen, to fasten on him the complete accountability for the death of Shomler, even though they had all seen that Shomler had acted independently and foolishly. Still, Tobblen had been nominally in charge, and everything that occurred on the hunt, whether good or bad, was the responsibility of the day's leader.

About fifty yards farther across the plain, the first line flushed another small wasp like the one Pura had killed. Once more Tobblen and the others waited while the first line hunted it down and killed it. Hanest decided to leave its dead body on the plain; the first wasp had supplied more than enough to replace the materials used on the day's hunt, and the huge wasp from the day before would provide materials for the entire community for weeks to come. Stripping this second small wasp would only encumber another hunter, and Hanest decided against it. They moved more carefully, aware that this part of the plain seemed to be riddled with freshly dug burrows of this unfamiliar subspecies of wasp.

The voices of the hunters were loud with friendly, confident chatter around Tobblen, but the men still avoided including him in their conversation. Tobblen's mood changed from depression to shame, and then to anger. He began to resent the others for their attitude; only the day before he had been a welcome member of their society, and he didn't believe that he had done anything to warrant his sudden exclusion. Not paying close attention to what was happening around him, still wrapped in his furious thoughts, Tobblen stumbled in a shallow hole. Something struck his foot as he lifted it out of the depression; among the short gray blades of grass, dull black wasp eyes stared at Tobblen. It was even smaller than the morning's two previous insects.

"Don't," said a voice in Tobblen's head.

"What?" thought Tobblen. He raised his spear as the wasp tried to burrow back into its ruined hole. Tobblen struck the insect with the haft of his spear, stunning the wasp. As he raised his spear to kill the wasp, the voice returned. "Don't," it said. Tobblen hesitated. He knew that it was the wasp, speaking in his mind.

"You have it?" called Hanest.

"Huh?" said Tobblen.

Hanest seemed exasperated. "Wake up, Tobblen," he shouted. "Is it dead?"

Tobblen looked down. The wasp was recovering already. The youth moved back a few steps. Suddenly, his mind was filled with an intense, paralyzing feeling of well-being. "Don't," said the wasp.

"Sure," called Tobblen. "It's plenty dead. I wonder how

many of these things there are around here." By now the wasp had disappeared under the ground.

"There's no way of knowing," said Hanest. "We'll take it slow for a while. Watch your step, now. Let's find some food."

"Thanks to you, human," whispered the wasp in Tobblen's mind.

The flood of pleasure was receding. "I don't know," said Tobblen. "I don't know what's happening."

The hunters returned to the copse several hours later, with enough meat to last the community for several days. There would be no hunting for a while, and Tobblen was grateful. He was very tired, and still angry. The women avoided him, too, just as their husbands had done. Darkai took their portion of meat and began preparing their meal. Tobblen lay back inside their shelter and thought about the day's events. He remembered the strange experience he had had with the wasp. He wondered if he ought to tell Darkai about that.

They ate the meal in silence. Several times during the evening Tobblen tried to begin a conversation, trying to break through his wife's irritating behavior. "All right," he said at one point, "I can almost understand why the other men on the hunt gave me that treatment. But at least they know, down underneath they know that it wasn't my fault. And then the women gave me the same thing only worse, because they weren't even there. They got everything from their men, at second hand. So they have nothing but stories to base their emotions on. But you, I can't understand it. You're my wife, Darkai. You're not just a casual neighbor. You can't feel comfortable in the rituals." She wouldn't answer even this, and she refused to meet his eyes when he demanded a reply. Darkai took her food outside and ate alone.

Some time later, after Tobblen had finished eating and prepared his weapons for the next hunt, whenever that should be announced, he took Darkai by the hand and led her angrily to their shelter. "That's enough," he said, shoving her to the bough-covered floor within. "I don't care if you won't talk. Maybe that's the best thing that you could do for me. But you're still my wife." He stripped the clothing from her roughly; she cried and made soft, frightened noises in her throat. He held her down, but she would not yield to him. Tobblen was furious. He raised one hand to strike her, but suddenly his rage and his desire left him. He stared at her for several seconds. She still would not look at him directly; she sobbed quietly to herself, her legs closed tightly together, her arms hugging her body. "You win, Darkai," said Tobblen through clenched teeth. "It always seemed like you were doing me a favor, anyway." He stretched out uncomfortably at one end of the shelter and tried to relax.

Soon Darkai went out and banked the cooking fire. The darkness deepened within the shelter. Tobblen was cold and very tired. He was glad that he could sleep as long as he wanted the next day, but he knew that a few extra hours of sleep would not heal the sickness he felt. He did not change position for a very long time, and he did not fall asleep. After a while he heard Darkai return. She did not come near him, but settled down in the far end of the shelter.

The sounds of the settlement quieted as the night came on. There were few night noises; at least, there were few that were unusual enough for Tobblen to notice. He realized that he was probably alone among the humans still awake, except the six people on watch. He rolled over on his back and sighed.

He began to be aware of a warm glow in his mind, a kind of fundamental satisfaction. It was a welcome change from the tortured thoughts of the previous hours. Still, Tobblen wasn't completely contented. He wondered if it was only drowsiness that caused his change in mood. A voice spoke in his mind and startled him. "Thanks to you, human," it said. Tobblen swore under his breath, but he did not move.

"Where are you?" he thought.

"I am on the plain, human," said the wasp. "I am in my burrow."

"Leave me alone," said Tobblen.

"You enjoy this," said the wasp. The feeling in Tobblen's mind increased, became a sense of fulfillment that left him no opportunity to question. The feeling continued to strengthen, and then to change. From a vague feeling of confidence, it became more purely pleasure-oriented. Tobblen felt his body grow aroused. His breathing came faster, more ragged. The feeling in his head took complete possession of him. For a time he was helpless, as his hips moved rhythmically and his head thrashed about in the consuming ecstasies the wasp dictated. It was a much more violent, more acute experience than any he had ever known with a woman; there were no mitigating elements involved, no concern with pleasing another person to distract him, no guilts, no awareness of the uncomfortable surroundings, no tinges of fatigue or other subordinate bodily wants. The pleasure was not associated in Tobblen's body, where the level of enjoyment might change from moment to moment. It was all directed immediately to his mind, bypassing the faulty recording devices of his senses. He moaned, though he did not realize it, and his hands dug through the layer of boughs that was his mattress, until his stiff fingers tried to grab hold of the packed dirt of the shelter's floor. At last he shrieked and cried, then quieted down gradually. The feeling in his mind subdued. He became aware of himself again; his body was hot and slippery with sweat, his belly and thighs sticky with his semen. Darkai was kneeling by his side, her expression unreadable in the faint light from outside the shelter.

"What," said Tobblen in a hoarse voice. "Did you . . . ?"

Darkai shook her head and went back to her corner of the shelter. Tobblen lay in the dark, panting. His mind cleared, and he recalled the voice of the wasp coming to him again. He shuddered when he remembered what the insect had just done to him. It had been an overpowering thing, yes, but still Tobblen felt violated. He felt filthy.

He crawled out of the shelter, carrying his clothes in one hand. Outside, he stood up and looked around. No one else was awake. The grove was peaceful; an illusion of security filled the settlement at nightfall, when the vast prairie and its terrors were invisible beyond the boles of the protecting trees. Tobblen walked slowly toward the small stream that ran through the copse, which watered the trees themselves and the humans as well. There would be a guard by the water, he knew, who would watch to see that any nocturnal predator that might come to drink would not satisfy any of its other needs at the humans' expense. Tobblen threw down his clothes on the edge of the stream and waded in. At its deepest, the water came only to mid-thigh. He knelt in the cold water and tried to scrub the interior stains away.

"All right, there," called the guard, a woman's voice. "Who's there?"

"It's me. Tobblen."

According to the rules, the guard was supposed to answer back, letting Tobblen know that the guard understood Tobblen was not an animal to be attacked, and that all was well by the water. Instead, the guard kept silent and turned away. It seemed to Tobblen that the woman was quitting her post, giving the youth up to whatever beast might happen by. Tobblen swore loudly, but got no response.

"Thanks to you, human," said the wasp, in Tobblen's mind.

"Leave me alone," said Tobblen, shuddering again.

"You were very pleased," said the wasp. "You will not hurt me. On the plain. When you hunt."

"If I see you, you're dead," said Tobblen.

"You will not kill me. You will not hurt me. You will not hurt my mates."

"Leave me alone."

"You enjoyed it, human. You want it, human. I will be back."

Tobblen's eyes filled with tears. He took a couple of handfuls of sand and rubbed his body until it stung. It did nothing for the sickened feeling he had inside. At last he left the water and put on his clothes. Then he went back to the shelter; he slept only fitfully, and his dreams were unpleasant.

In the morning he awoke slowly, his eyes bleary and his muscles cramped. Darkai was sitting out by the fire, drinking tea. Tobblen joined her there and sat for a moment before he spoke. "Are you going to talk to me today?" he asked at last.

"I'll talk to you, I suppose," she said, still not looking at him.

"That's progress, at least," said Tobblen angrily. He stood up again and walked to the small congregation area of the grove, a clear space in the center of the community dominated by the death tree and the large cabin of the leaders. There were several men and women standing idly against the front wall of the cabin, and other people coming and going through the congregation area. Tobblen walked boldly toward the group of hunters. "Feels good, not to have to go out today, doesn't it?" he said, his voice hard and aggressive. The men and women continued their conversation without even a slight hesitation. One woman yawned, a man spit on the ground, but not one of them acknowledged Tobblen's presence. "How much more?" Tobblen shouted. "What do you want me to do?" He didn't get an answer, and he just stared for a moment. Then, furious, he turned and went back to his shelter.

The day passed slowly for him. There was nothing that he could do; no one in the community would permit him to join in their work or entertainment. The pressure and the shame grew in him, until he wondered how he could even bear to live with it. Darkai spoke to him, but Tobblen realized that even that was a breaking of the unspoken law. Nevertheless, her tone was impersonal, with none of her former affection. When he tried to caress her that night she repulsed him. Once more she went to sleep in a corner of the shelter, as far from him as she could position herself.

"I am here again, human. Thanks to you." Tobblen started in the darkness that night, when he heard the familiar voice in his head.

"Go away." He felt a peculiar mixture of desire and loathing, of utter lustful craving and disgust.

"No," said the wasp. "You do not want me to go. Listen." The insect said nothing more, not in words. But Tobblen's mind began to seek out the first tinges of warmth, as he had felt the night before. Soon they became apparent. As the minutes passed, the feeling grew in him.

"Yes," whispered Tobblen, damning his own helplessness. Already he was covered with sweat in anticipation. "I'll stop it, this time," he said. "I'll let it go part way, and then I'll stop it." Just then the wasp intensified the feeling. Tobblen did no more thinking for a long while. His body was wracked with the almost painful pleasure, the deep, completely voluptuous gratification. He rolled onto his back, sobbing and moaning, oblivious to everything in his world but the mental rapture that the monstrous insect imposed on him. At last it was over, and the ravishment ended, and the feeling of contentment evaporated. As Tobblen's senses returned to him, he felt a growing nausea, as much from his knowledge of the source of his pleasures as from his total inability to resist them.

"You will not harm me," said the wasp. "You will not harm my mates."

Tobblen was possessed now by horror and hatred, where just moments before he had known desire. "I will kill you," he said.

"On your hunt, this thing can happen to you."

The youth imagined what a disaster that could be. This new variety of wasp was more of a threat than even the huge killer types.

"Leave me alone." Tobblen's tone was pleading.

"Thanks to you, human," said the wasp. "You enjoy it."

When morning came, Tobblen was still awake. He had worried away the entire night. He had decided to give the community one final chance; he knew that he had a kind of power, in that he understood the threat these new wasps represented. The knowledge was a weapon that might be used to strike down the others' treatment of him. Darkai was sullen once more when she awoke. "You'll have to cheer up," he told her. "You'll have to dig up some of that old love. For your own good."

"Shomler was my brother," she said bitterly.

"And I'm your husband."

"Go see what Shomler's widow has to say about husbands," said Darkai.

"Naelly?" Tobblen laughed. "I thought I saw two pair of feet sticking out of old Shomler's place the other night, and he's not even cold in the ground yet." Darkai turned and walked away. Tobblen shrugged and went to the congregation area. The group of hunters had another day of liberty. They noticed him briefly as he approached, but still refused to speak to him. "Listen," he said, "there's danger on the plain. New danger. I saw it the other day. If you're not going to talk to me, you won't find out about it." They made no reaction at all, continuing their discussion of the probable weather for the next day's hunt.

"All right," thought Tobblen. "That settles it. You can find out the hard way." He took some fishing gear from the leaders' cabin and wasted a few lonely hours by the water, upstream from the grove, about a hundred yards out on the plain. He caught nothing, but then he wasn't really trying. At suppertime he returned to his shelter and Darkai, but the meal was eaten in silence. The tension and the frustration were more than Tobblen could stand. He went into the shelter and entertained thoughts of vengeance. He planned to send Darkai away, when she came to see if he was all right. She did not come.

"Wasp," thought Tobblen.

"I am here, human."

"I want you, wasp."

"Thanks to you, human."

Tobblen felt the initial traces of sensual pleasure enter his mind. The wasp did not linger over the first stages, this time; the entire process was shorter, though no less intense. The wasp left his mind at last, and Tobblen was exhausted. Once again he was left filled with loathing, both of the insect and of his own lack of resolution. The feeling of repugnance and disease grew, and with a cry of anguish Tobblen realized that he could be rid of neither. He hit the ground helplessly, and sobbed. Darkai paid no attention. Tobblen crawled from the shelter, his thoughts confused. He staggered a few steps and then collapsed, where he vomited repeatedly until he was too weak even to kneel. He lost consciousness there, lying in a pool of his own vomit, and he awoke hours later, after sunset, and realized that Darkai had let him remain where he had fallen.

The night was dark, as the day had been, overcast and moonless. Tobblen stood up. His head was clear now, and his legs weren't shaky at all, after a few steps. He wandered down to the stream and cleansed the stale, crusty stuff from his face and chest, and from his clothes. Then he wondered what he ought to do. He stood there for a few minutes, thinking. He turned back to look toward the shelters, the only home he had ever known, though now they didn't seem as warm and protective any longer. He turned again and walked to the leaders' cabin, where the weapons and tools were stored. He took two spears, feeling no twinge of guilt at robbing the community. Then he walked through the sleeping settlement, unchallenged by the guards, and stepped out onto the dark plain.

He had never before been on the plain this late after sundown. It was a dangerous and foolish thing to do, but in his present mood Tobblen didn't especially care. He headed toward the horizon, in the direction he knew best from the hunts, and avoided the dangers with which he was familiar. "Goodbye, wasp," he thought.

"Thanks to you, human," came the wasp's voice in his mind. "Goodbye. We will find another human."

"It won't be any trouble, I'm sure," thought Tobblen. "That's one of the bad things about people. We're all expendable, even here." There was no further reply from the wasp. Tobblen laughed bitterly to himself. He had even been abandoned by the insect.

He marched most of the night, until he knew that he was in unknown territory. Then he slowed almost to a halt, progressing carefully across the spiky grass, searching for dangers. As the sun rose, Tobblen began to feel tired. There was no shelter available, so he sat down in the gray weeds and dozed, knowing that he was vulnerable to any kind of enemy. He still didn't especially care. He took up his journey later and continued on in this way, stopping when he was weary, killing small animals when he was hungry, eating them uncooked, bearing a growing thirst until he happened on a small creek running across his path. And all the time he thought. He realized that survival meant something different than he had been taught. He had always assumed that it was the strongest that survived; the beast with the most power, or the swiftest legs. No, there was a difference between being strong and being fit. Certainly, human beings were stronger than most of the animals that dwelled on the plain, but they were not, in their present situation, *fit* to live in security.

Then, with a shock, Tobblen realized what his former friends had done to him. Like Shomler, he had been driven out, weeded out, from their midst. Shomler was unfit as a hunter; he was killed. And Tobblen had proven himself unfit to accept the kind of mental strain under which he'd have to perform, one way or another, for the rest of his life. He, too, had cracked and left the community, and Darkai and the rest would no doubt be saddened but glad to know they were the better for it.

"But they don't understand," thought Tobblen, as tears ran down his face. "They don't know about the wasp. It wasn't just their attitude. That was just a test, I know. That I could have put up with. It was the wasp. The wasp." Sobbing, Tobblen fell to his knees. After a time, he made an effort to gain control of himself. He stood again, and resumed his march. "They were right, then," he thought. "I'm not fit."

Some time later he saw a blur on the horizon. Approaching cautiously, he saw that it was a stand of micha trees. He crawled within a hundred yards, silently, invisible on the gray plain. There was a stream cutting across the plain, perhaps the same that he had drunk from hours before. A young woman was washing some clothing in the water. She was singing, and her voice came faintly to Tobblen's ears. "Oh, no," he thought. "What do I do now? I could join them, claiming that I was a wanderer from a hunting party destroyed by wasps. I could pretend to be starving and half-mad, and then they would take me in and nurse me. Then I could begin again. From the start. All over."

"We are here, too, human," came a wasp's voice. "Wherever you are, we shall be. Thanks to you, human."

Tobblen cried out. His arms felt weak as he held himself up to observe the young woman, and he collapsed and sobbed. The young woman hadn't heard him, and couldn't see his tortured convulsions of despair. After a while, Tobblen rose and turned his back on the human settlement. Then he walked out blindly across the endless gray plain.

Enjoy, Enjoy

Frederik Pohl

If we are visited on Earth by aliens whose technology is far greater than ours, what will we have to offer them in exchange for their friendship? Frederik Pohl tells a characteristically acerbic story of a man who was given a job by aliens. His duties? Simply to enjoy himself, as much as possible for as long as possible. But that, as we all know, isn't as easy as we'd like it to be.

Frederik Pohl has been hailed by Kingsley Amis as the best writer in science fiction. He's probably best known for his collaborations with the late C. M. Kornbluth—including The Space Merchants *and* Gladiator-at-Law—*but he continues to write excellent stories by himself, including the recent novella* The Gold at the Starbow's End.

Booze, broads, big cars, the finest of food, waterbeds filled with vintage champagne. Those were some of the things that went with Tud Cowpersmith's job. The way he got the job was by going to a party in Jackson Heights. The way he happened to be at the party was that he had no choice.

It wasn't a bad party, for a loft in Jackson Heights. It wasn't a bad loft. The windows at one end looked out on the tracks of the IRT el, but they had been painted over with acrylics to look like stained glass. Every twenty minutes you got a noise like some very large person stumbling by with garbage-can lids for shoes, but except for that the el might as well not have been there. Anyway at that end of the loft the stereo speakers stood four feet high on the floor, so the noise didn't matter all that much. You couldn't possibly talk at that end. Cowpersmith wanted, eventually, to talk, as soon as the person he wanted to talk to showed up, so he drifted to the other end.

There the noise was more or less bearable, and there the windows were still clear. They were even clean. He could see through them down on a sort of communal garden, three or four backyards for three or four different old apartment buildings thrown together: a tiny round plastic swimming pool, now iced over with leaves and boughs frozen into it; bare trees that probably had looked very nice in the summer. To get to the windows at that end you had to thread your way through a sort of indoor jungle, potted plants presumably carried in from the garden for the cold weather. And there, on a chrome-rimmed, chrome-legged kitchen table, the host and hostess were rolling joints. They greeted Cowpersmith—

"Want a hit?"

"Thanks."

—but the pot did not ease him. He was looking for somebody. That was the reason he was there.

The person he was looking for was named Murray. Murray was an old, old . . . friend? Something like that. What he basically was was somebody who owed Cowpersmith fifty dollars, from a time when fifty hadn't seemed like an awful lot. Cowpersmith had heard, the day before, that Murray was in town, and tracked him down to a hotel on Central Park South.

After some deliberation he had telephoned Murray. He really hated doing it. He needed the fifty, but in his view the odds against getting it were so bad that he didn't like the risk of investing a dime in a phone call. The dime was, after all, real money. There was no way to flash a revoked American Express card at the phone booth, as he had done with the last two restaurants and the airline that had brought him back from Chicago, where the last of his bankroll had melted away. But the odds had paid off! Murray was in, and obliging—

"What fifty?"

"Well, don't you remember, you met that Canadian girl—"

"Oh, Christ, sure. Was it only fifty? Must be some interest due by now, Tud. Tell you what—"

—and the way it worked out they were to meet at this party, and Cowpersmith would collect not fifty but a hundred dollars.

That required some decision making, too, because there was the investment for a subway token to be considered. But Murray had sounded prosperous enough for a gamble. Only no Murray. Cowpersmith took another hit from a girl wearing batik bellbottoms and a halter top and glared around the room. Through the roar of Alice Cooper he realized she was talking to him.

"What?"

"I said, is your name Ted?"

"Tud."

"Turd?"

"Tud Cowpersmith," he yelled over the androgynous rock. "It's a family name, Tudsbury."

She reached up close to his ear—she was not more than five feet tall—and shouted, "If you're a friend of Murray's he's looking for you." He allowed her to lead him around the buttress of the stairwell, for the first time noticing that her armpits were unshaven, the hair on her head stuck out in tiny, tied witch curls and she was quite pretty.

And there was Murray, knotting his wild red eyebrows hospitably. "Hey, Tud. Looking great, man! Long time."

"You're looking fine too," said Cowpersmith, although it wasn't really true. Murray looked a little bit fine and a lot prosperous; the medallion that hung over his raw-silk shirt was clearly gold, and he wore a very expensive-looking, though ugly, thick wristwatch. The thing was he also looked about fifteen years older than he had eighteen months before. They sat in two facing armchairs, one a broken lounger, the other so overstuffed that the stuffing was curling out of it. The girl sat crosslegged between them on the floor, and Murray idly played with her tied curls.

Cooper had changed to the New York Queens and somebody had turned the volume down, or else the shelter of the stairwell did the same thing for them. Cowpersmith got several words of what Murray was saying.

"A job?" Cowpersmith repeated. "What kind of a job?"

"The finest fucking job in all the world," said Murray, and laughed and laughed, poking the girl's shoulder. When he had calmed down, he said, "What do you work for, Tud?"

Cowpersmith said angrily, "God, *you* know. I worked for the advertising agency until they took cigarette ads off TV, then I was with the oil company until—"

"No, no. For what *purpose*."

Cowpersmith shrugged. "Money?"

"Sure, but what do you do with the money?"

"Pay bills?" he guessed.

"No, no, damn it! *After* you do all the lousy stuff like that.

What do you do with the *extra* money? Like when you were still pulling down twenty-five K at the agency and everything was on the expense account anyway?"

"Oh, sure." It had been so long ago Cowpersmith had almost forgotten. "Fun. Good food. Plays. Girls. Cars—"

"Right on," cried Murray, "and that's what everyone else works for, too. Everybody but me! That's what my job *is*. I don't have to work *for* those things, because I work *at* them. I don't imagine you're going to believe this, Tud, but it's true," he added as an afterthought.

Cowpersmith looked down at the girl and swallowed hard. A dismal vision flashed through his mind, of the five crumpled twenties in his pocket turning out to be joke money that, turned over, might say *April Fool* or, held for ten minutes, might evaporate their ink leaving bare paper and ruin. "I don't have any idea of what you're talking about," he said to Murray, but still looking at the girl.

"You think I'm stoned," Murray said accurately.

"Well—"

"I don't blame you. Look. Well, let's see. Shirley," he said, half-laughing, "how do we explain this? Try it this way," he went on, not waiting for her help, "suppose you had all the money in the world. Suppose you had more money than you even wanted, right?"

"I follow you. I mean, as a theoretical thing."

"And then suppose you had like an accident. Crash-bang; you're in a car accident or a piano falls on you. Quadriplegic. Can't have any fun any more. Got that?"

"Bad scene," said Cowpersmith, nodding.

"All right, but even though you can't do much yourself any more, there's a way you can have *some* fun vicariously. Like you're not going to Ibiza yourself, but you're seeing slides of it, or something. You can't get the kicks a normal person can, but you can get something, maybe not much but better than nothing, out of what other people do. Now, in that position, Tud, what would you do?"

"Kill myself."

"No you wouldn't, for Christ's sake. You'd hire other people to have fun for you. And then with this process—" he patted the ugly thing that looked like a wristwatch, but Cowpersmith now realized was not—"you can play back their fun, and maybe it isn't much but it's all the jollies you can ever get. Right, Shirley?"

She shook her head and said sweetly, "Shit."

"Well, anyway, it's *something* like that. I guess. It's kind of secret, I think probably because it's someone like Howard Hughes or maybe one of the Rockefellers that's involved. They won't say. But the job's for real, Tud. All I have to do is have all the fun I can. They pick up the tab, it all goes on the credit card, and they get the bill, and they pay it. As long as I wear this thing that's all I have to do. And every Friday, besides all that, five hundred in cash."

There was a pause, while Bette Midler flowed over and around them from the speakers and Cowpersmith looked from the girl to his friend, waiting for the joke part. At last he said, "But *nobody* gets a job like that."

"Wrong, friend," said Shirley. "You did. Just now. If you want it. I'll take you there tomorrow morning."

Behind the door stenciled *E.T.C. Import-Export Co., Ltd.* there was nothing more than a suite of offices sparsely occupied and eccentrically furnished. Hardly furnished at all, you might say. There was nobody at the reception desk, which Shirley walked right past, and no papers on the desk of the one man anywhere visible. "I've got a live one for you, Mr. Morris," Shirley sang out. "Friend of Murray's."

Mr. Morris looked like a printing salesman, about fifty, plump, studying Cowpersmith over half-glasses. "Good producer," he agreed reluctantly. "All right, you're hired."

And he counted out five hundred dollars in bills of various sizes and pushed them across the desk to Cowpersmith.

Cowpersmith picked up the money, feeling instantly stoned. "Is that all there is to it?"

"No! Not for me, I've got all the paperwork now, your credit card, keeping records—"

"I mean, like, don't you want me to fill out an application form?"

"Certainly not." He opened his desk drawer and pulled out a wristwatch-shaped thing. Cowpersmith could not see all of the inside of the drawer from his angle, but he was nearly sure there was nothing else in it. He handed it to Cowpersmith and said, "Once you put it on it won't come off by itself, but we'll unlock it any time you want to quit. That's all. Go have fun. By which," he added, "I don't actually mean screwing, because we've got plenty of records of that already."

"What then?" asked Cowpersmith, disconcerted.

"Hell, man! Up to you. Water skiing, skin diving, breaking the bank at Monte Carlo. What do you dream about, when things look bad? You do dream, don't you?"

"Well, sure, but—" Cowpersmith hesitated, thinking. "I always wanted to eat at *La Tour d'Argent*. And, uh, there's this crazy poison fish they have in Japan—"

"Sounds good," the man said without enthusiasm. "I'll have your card delivered to you at your hotel tomorrow."

"Yes, but wait a minute. What's the catch?"

"No catch, Tud," said Shirley, annoyed. "Jesus, what does it take to convince you?"

"Nothing like this ever happened to me before. There has to be something wrong with it."

"No there doesn't," said Mr. Morris, "and I have to get busy on your card."

Cowpersmith found himself standing up. "No, wait," he said. "How—how long does the job last?"

Shrug. "Until you get bored, I guess."

"Then what?"

"Then you turn in your recordings. And you take your last week's pay and go look for another job."

"Recordings?" Cowpersmith looked down at his wrist, where, without thinking about it, he had clasped on the metal object. "Is this a tape recorder?"

"I'm not into that part of it," Mr. Morris said. "I only know my job, and I've just done it. Goodbye."

And that was all she wrote. At Shirley's urging, Cowpersmith checked into a small but very nice hotel on the Upper East Side, went to a massage parlor, ice-skated at Rockefeller Center, and met Shirley for a late drink in a Greek bar in Chelsea. "Good start," she said. "Now you're on your own. Got any plans?"

"Well," he said experimentally, "I think I can still make the Mardi Gras in Rio. And I heard about a safari tour to Kenya—"

"Travel, huh. Why not?" She finished her drink. "Well, we'll keep in touch—"

"No, take it easy," he said. "I don't understand some things."

"There isn't any reason for you to understand. Just enjoy."

"I tried to call Murray, but he's gone off somewhere—"

"And you're going too, right? Look," she said, "you're going to ask some probably very important questions, to you, but all I know's my own job—"

"Which is?"

"—which is none of your business. Go enjoy. When Mr. Morris wants to be in touch with you he'll be in touch with you. No. Don't ask how he'll find you. He'll find you. And so good night."

And so, for eight dynamite months, Tud Cowpersmith enjoyed. He did everything he had ever wanted to do. He made the carnival in Rio and discovered hearts-of-palm soup in a restaurant overlooking the Copacabana beach. He rode a hydrofoil around Leningrad and toured the Hermitage, bloated on fresh caviar. Gypsy violins in Soho, pounded abalone on Fisherman's Wharf, a nude-encounter weekend at Big Sur, high-stakes gambling in Macao. First-class stewardesses on half a dozen airlines began to recognize him, in half a dozen languages. Shirley turned up once, in his suite at the George Cinq, but only to tell him he was doing fine. Another time he thought he saw Murray pushing a scooter at the Copenhagen airport, but he was going one way and Murray another and there was no way for Cowpersmith to get off the moving person-carrier to catch him. He took up motorcycle racing and tried to enjoy listening to the harpsichord and, in spite of what Morris had said, repeatedly and enthusiastically enjoyed a great deal of sex. It was at the time of his second case of gonorrhea that he began to feel enough was very nearly enough, and then one morning his phone rang.

"Cowpersmith?" said Mr. Morris' tinny little voice, very far away. "You don't seem to be having a lot of fun right now. Are you about ready to quit?"

Although the pleasure had not been quite as much pleasure lately, the prospect of losing it was very much pain. "No!" yelped Cowpersmith. "What are you talking about? Hell, man, you should see the girl I just—" He looked around; he was alone in the big bed. "I mean, I've got this date—"

"No," whispered the small voice, "that's not good enough.

Your EI's been down for three weeks now. Not below the threshhold yet. We can still get a little good stuff from you. But the quality's definitely down, Cowpersmith, and something's got to be done about it."

Dismayed, Cowpersmith sat up and swung his feet over the side of the bed. "How do you know about—what is it, my EI?"

"Emotional index? Well, what do you think, man? We continuously monitor the product, and it just isn't what we want."

"Yeah," Cowpersmith conceded. "Look, I just woke up and I'm a little fuzzy, but—" He got out of bed, carrying the phone, and sat in a chair by the window. Outside was Grosvenor Square, with a demonstration going on in front of the American Embassy, so he knew he was in the Europa in London.

"But what, Cowpersmith?"

"But I'll think of something. Hold on."

By this time the staff of the hotel had learned to value him and understand his likes, so the floor waiter, alerted by the incoming phone call, was bringing in his black coffee, American style, with two large glasses of fresh orange juice. Cowpersmith swallowed a little of one and a little of the other and said, "Listen, can you give me an idea of what he likes?"

"Who likes?"

"Whoever it is is paying for all this stuff."

"I can't discuss our clients," said Mr. Morris. "They told me not to."

"Well, can you give me some idea?"

"No. I don't know what you've been doing; the monitor doesn't show that. It shows where you are and how you're feeling. That's it. We won't know exactly what you've been up to until the debriefing, when they study the recordings. Me, I'll never know. Not my department."

"Well, don't you have *any* idea what kind of stuff they like?"

"Mostly, any kind of stuff they haven't had before."

"Hah!" Cowpersmith thought wildly. "Listen, how's this? Has anybody just sort of sat and meditated for you?"

Pause. "You mean like religious meditation? Like some kind of guru?"

"Well, yes. Or just sitting and thinking, like, you know, Thoreau at Walden Pond."

"I give it forty-eight hours," said Mr. Morris.

"Or—well, how about skin diving? Again. The doctor told me to lay off for a little while until my ear healed up after Bermuda, but I heard about this neat stuff at the Great Barrier Reef, and—"

"Cowpersmith," said the tiny voice, "you know what you're costing? Not counting the half a thousand a week in cash. Your charge has been running over forty-eight hundred a week, on the average. You got to show more than some spearfishing maybe a couple weeks from now. You got to show *today*. *And* tomorrow. And every day. So long."

So Cowpersmith kept at it. The meditation didn't seem to be going well after the first hour, so he hired a new travel consultant and for a while things looked bright. Or bright enough. Maybe. He backpacked across the Trinity Mountains and flew to Naples for a swim in the Blue Grotto. He ate couscous and drank akvavit and smoked Acapulco gold, all in their native environment. Then he took a pack mule through the Montana hills, and flew back to Naples for four hours of clambering around the ruins of Pompeii, and hit Paris for nightclubs and Waikiki for surfing . . .

. . . But a couple of wipeouts at Diamond Head made his ear feel worse, and one nightclub turned out to be an awful lot like another, except that where the toilet jokes were in French he couldn't understand them. He knew the phone was going to ring again. He didn't need the little machine on his wrist to tell him he was down. He *felt* down.

So he came to a decision, and just sat in his hotel room, sullenly waiting. He had already put eleven thousand dollars in a numbered bank account in Bern and paid off all his old debts, and if it was over it was over.

But he didn't want it to be over.

The more he thought about it, the more he didn't want it to be over.

It was, after all, the finest fucking job in all the world, and everything Murray had said about it was true. No more head-waiters falling all over themselves? No more pretty women to take to the clubs, to the tracks, to bed? He ordered up a couple of bottles of brandy and worked himself up to a weeping drunk and when, the next morning, it was inevitably followed by a dry-mouthed, burning-bellied hangover he sat wallowing in the misery of his thousand-franc-a-day suite, shaking and enfeebled, barely moving to order up food, and more booze, and more food. The longer he sat the worse he felt. And the next day. And the next day. And—

And by the fifth day, after most of a week of solid, sullen misery, he realized that his phone had not rung.

Why not? He certainly wasn't enjoying.

He didn't understand why, but when it came through to his mind that it was so he didn't really care why. Hope was back. The magic money machine had not turned itself off! So he cleaned himself up. He got himself dressed. He waved off the floor waiter and the major-domo and the concierge and went out for a walk, a perfectly dull, uninteresting, unexciting walk, up the Champs Elysees to the Lido Arcade. He ate a quiche and drank a beer and dropped in on a flick. It was an old

Barbra Streisand with French subtitles; he had seen it before and he didn't care. It bored the ears off him. He enjoyed being bored very much.

But when he got back to the hotel, New York was on the line.

"For homey pleasures," said Mr. Morris' small, distant voice, "you don't get paid this kind of money. You want a McDonald's hamburger, quit and come back."

"I had this feeling you'd call," Cowpersmith acknowledged. "What can I say? I've had it with joy. It is no fun any more."

"So quit. This was your second warning anyhow, and you don't get but three."

"All right," said Cowpersmith, after a moment of digesting that bit of information. "But tell me one thing. Last week I was *really* down, how come you didn't fire me then?"

"Last week? Last week you were *great*. I thought you knew, pleasure isn't the only sensation they like."

"You mean you'll pay me for misery?"

"One of our best units," said the little voice in his ear, "was terminal stomach cancer. They paid him five grand a week plus full medical every week he didn't take painkillers."

That took a moment to digest too, and it went down hard, but Cowpersmith began to see hope. "Well, I don't want to go that far—"

"Whatever you were doing last week was far enough, I'd say."

"Then maybe I could—"

"Sure," said Mr. Morris. "Nice talking to you. Third strike is out."

Ensued some of the most depressing weeks of Cowpersmith's life. Not miserable. At least not reliably miserable; he could not even be sure, from day to day, that he was quite bugged enough to register a decent misery on his wristband, and that in itself was discouraging. He tried everything he

could think of. Inspiration struck and he made a quick list
of all the things he had been putting off because they were
awful: went to the dentist, had a barium enema, got tattooed.
That took care of three days, and, looking back at them honestly, he had to admit they were not memorably bad, merely
lousy. He flew back to Washington and spent two afternoons
in the Senate gallery—merely tedious; after the first half-hour
he stopped hearing what was being said and caught himself
drowsing off. He flanged together two stereo systems and
poured thirty watts of acid rock into one earpiece and Mahler
into the other and came out with only a headache. He in-
vented excuses to go in and out of Kennedy airport, with
special emphasis on the Customs line and the hackstands,
but after a while even that anger diminished. Food. Remembering all the enjoyment he had had from good food, he
looked for dyspepsia and displeasure from bad. He ate a
haggis in Glasgow, flew to Heathrow and had brawn for dinner, caught a commuter flight to Paris and had an American
breakfast at Orly. None of it worked very well. It proved to be
harder to make oneself unhappy than to find joy, which had,
after all, lasted for the best part of a year. The other thing was
that deliberately making oneself unhappy made one, well,
unhappy. It was not a way he liked to live. He discovered that
twenty cups of coffee a day, sixty cigarettes, and a maximum
of three hours of sleep gave him a perpetual headachey feeling
that made everything an annoyance, but the other side of the
coin was that nothing was much *more* than an annoyance; he
was simply too beat to care. In desperation he returned to the
States and delved into copies of the underground press, answering all the ads he could find for "instruction," "disci-
pline," and so on, but that mostly got him a large number of
FBI men and postal inspectors, and the S-M experiences
were basically, he thought, pretty God-awful anyway. So he
was not all that surprised when, less than five weeks from the

second warning, his phone rang again. He was in Waikiki, where he had been nerving himself up to trying to get his ear hurting again in the surf, and he was frankly grateful to be spared it.

"Third time's the charm," said the little voice. "Come home, come home for debriefing."

"I'm fired, right?"

"Well," said distant Mr. Morris judiciously, "you stop working for us as soon as you're debriefed. But you get a year's severance pay, which comes to, let's see, twenty-six K."

"Wow!" cried Cowpersmith. And then, "Uh. Say. Was that, you know, just to give me a high?"

"No, although you did register a beaut. No, it's real. You just have to turn over the recording, and you're on your own."

"Well," said Cowpersmith, picking up the phone and walking out onto the lanai. "Well," he said, surrendering a dream, "I guess that's about it, then. Isn't it? I'll catch the first plane tomorrow—"

"No," said Mr. Morris, "you won't do that, you'll catch the next plane right now. We've arranged for your tickets, they'll be at the desk when you check out. Which should be in fifteen minutes."

And five minutes after he hung up, the Ilikai bellman was at the door, eager for Cowpersmith's one beaten bag.

Mr. Morris had been very thorough. They not only had Cowpersmith's ticket at the desk, they had an envelope with two twenty-dollar bills and ten singles, for tips and miscellaneous. And they also had their instructions about his credit card. "I'm very sorry," said the clerk politely, "but as of the time you settle your account with us your card is canceled. And we have to pick it up. It's part of our contract with the company—"

"Well, fine," said Cowpersmith. "Tell you what. I forgot

to pick up a couple little things in the shops, so let me have the card for a minute *before* I finish settling up."

"So sorry," said the clerk. "You already have."

And now, when it was all over, Cowpersmith spent his time in the taxi to the airport thinking of things he could have done, but had not. He got onto the plane in a daze of missed menus and untried wines, and had to be prodded sharply by the stewardess before he realized he was in the wrong part of the airplane. "Sorry," he mumbled, allowing himself to be led aft. He glanced around with some wonder. He had almost forgotten that there were parts of a 707 where people sat three abreast.

At Kennedy he was met: Shirley.

He stared at her through gummed eyelids. By the sun it was late afternoon, but by the clock of his body it was eight in the morning after a night with no more sleep than a man can get sitting in a coach seat between a fat plumber on a group tour and a small boy who alternated snoring and leaping about. "Had fun?" she asked, steering him toward a chauffeur-driven Bentley.

"You know better than I," he said bitterly, trying to take the wristband off and slap it in her palm. The gesture failed, because it still would not come open.

"You'll feel better when we get going," she said. "I've got a Thermos of coffee. It's about an hour's drive."

"I know, I know," grumped Cowpersmith, who had, after all, been in and out on the Kennedy-Manhattan run more times than he could count. But when the chauffeur took a right-hand turn where there had always been a left he realized he did not know. It did not seem important, and he drowsed until the car stopped, doors opened—

"Here's your boy, Morrie."

"Looks like we'll have to carry him in."

—and he opened his eyes to see Mr. Morris and the chauffeur tugging at him.

"I'm all right," he said with dignity, and halfway up the pebbled walk looked around and said. "Where is this place, anyway?" Porticoed porch, ivied walls, he had not seen it before.

"Where you get debriefed," said Shirley, pausing at the door. "So long, Tud."

He hesitated. "You're not coming in? Will I see you again?"

"I'll see you," she said, patted his shoulderblade and returned to the car.

Sensory impressions smote him: An entrance hall, with a staircase winding up under a huge canvas-shrouded painting in a gilt frame. A library of glassed-in shelves, mostly empty, with drop-clothed chairs around a cold and swept fireplace. A dining hall, and beyond it a closed door.

"Does he live in this place, whoever he is?" asked Cowpersmith, staring about.

Mr. Morris sighed. "There is 'no 'he,' " he said patiently. "There are 'they.' They are here, some of them . . . This is the part I hate," he added morosely.

"Why?"

"Well, you're going to ask a lot of questions again. You all do. And you're going to figure you've done your bit, now you have a right to know. Right? And maybe in a sense you do, although it's pretty pointless . . . Anyway. What we do now, we take the recordings from you, and when we've got enough to make a shipment we send them off. I don't know where, exactly. I don't know what they do with them, exactly. But it's a big business with them."

"Big business?" Misconceptions and erroneous assumptions were splintering in Cowpersmith's brain.

"Well, like a TV network. I mean, I think they kind of broadcast them, sort of like a *National Geographic* television special: sensory impressions from all over, strange pleasures of the aborigines—"

"I *never*," said Cowpersmith positively, apprehensions dissolving the sleep from his mind, "heard any broadcast like that."

"No. Not on this planet, no."

Cowpersmith swallowed, choking on apprehensions and the splinters of former certainties.

"The mistake you made," said Mr. Morris sympathetically, "is that you assumed the people who hired you were human beings. They're not. No. You wouldn't think so if you'd seen one. They, uh . . . Well, they look a little bit like fish and a little bit like the devil. All red, you see. And not very big—"

"But Murray said—"

"Oh, Christ," said Mr. Morris, "how would Murray know? If it's any consolation to you, when he was debriefed he was as surprised as you are. It gets everybody the same way."

"Bloody charming," said Cowpersmith bitterly. "Now I'm an agent of a foreign power. I wouldn't be surprised if the FBI picks me up about this."

"I would," said Mr. Morris. "In there, go on."

"Where?"

"There. Through the door."

"What do we do in there?" Cowpersmith demanded, truculent because the only alternative was being terrified.

"You turn over the recording to them and that's that," said Mr. Morris.

Cowpersmith swallowed again, choking this time on plain panic. He wished that the car hadn't gone away. Still, he thought, they had to be somewhere on Long Island. Maybe

Sands Point? Maybe Patchogue. And he still had most of the fifty dollars, plus whatever had been left in his coat, plus, of course, that Swiss bank account. There would be a taxi . . .

"Okay," he said, tugging at the wristband. "Let's get it over with and I'll get out of here."

"Oh," said Mr. Morris, annoyed, "what are you doing? That's not the recording. That's only the monitor, so we could tell how you were doing and where you were. You turn over the recording in there."

And he opened the door behind the dining hall.

Two men in white stepped through. They were not smiling. They were without expression, like saloon bouncers or dog catchers.

The room behind them looked like an operating chamber: bright lights over a flat white table. Rows of transparent jars lined the shelves around the room. They came in two sizes:

In the large (there were two of them) red and hideous things stirred uneasily, looking out toward Cowpersmith with great pale eyes.

In the smaller jars, of which there were more than a dozen—

Were the floating objects in them *really* human heads? And that one there, next to the brighter of the two red creatures, the one with the wild red eyebrows—wasn't it very familiar?

It was too late to turn; the men were reaching out for him as Mr. Morris said from behind him, sadly, disclaimingly, "What better recording could they have than the one in your own brain?"

The Stones Have Names

Mildred Downey Broxon

Humans in the mass are frequently insensitive to the depredations we visit on other forms of life—as witness our many current ecological crises. When we achieve star travel we may prove just as destructive to the beings who live on far planets. But there will always be individual humans who are capable of seeing the viewpoint of other creatures; "The Stones Have Names" is the story of one such man, and of the alien who becomes his friend.

Mildred Downey Broxon is a graduate of the Clarion Science Fiction Writers' Workshops; her stories have appeared in Clarion *and* Universe.

Twilight was falling, light purple on the water; I sat above the incoming tide, waiting for the new Terran governor. He was late, of course; it was the Terran way of showing us that their time was more important than ours.

I watched a wave reach higher than the rest to cover a colony of rock crusters. Grateful for the moisture, they snapped open and brandished tiny blue-tipped tentacles. Behind me, in the *tial*, our honored dead stirred and muttered in their sleep. Sunset; their time, soon. My mother Ilor lay there. What did she think of my guiding a Terran to our village?

"It's traditional now, Ilor," I told her, wondering if she could hear. "The new governor inspects the village, orders any changes he wants, then returns to the Terran compound for the rest of his stay. There's nothing I can do about it, anyhow. You tried, but the Terrans won. They always win."

I turned and looked down the path, past the *tial*. Night was coming, and Terrans hated the dark. Where was he? I rose and was about to leave when I saw a pale glimmer and heard footsteps. One set of footsteps. Had he come alone? I hurried to meet him.

He was walking slowly, picking his way in the gloom—their eyes are smaller than ours, and do not see well in dim light—brushing away branches, swatting at wingthings. Yes, he was alone, unless his guards were hiding. But Terrans are large and clumsy, and not skilled at hiding. I stepped forward and bowed.

"Greetings, honored sir," I said in his language. "Welcome to our village."

He jumped; evidently he had not seen me in the darkness. Our gray skins do blend well with shadows. "Oh. Yes. Thank you. I'm sorry I'm late, the damned aides kept insisting I needed an escort, and—"

I twitched my ears. A Terran, apologizing to a Calliur? "If you will accompany me, I will guide you to the village." As we left I could hear Ilor whispering in the *tial*. She spoke of betrayal, but the honored dead are often bitter. What could I do?

The path to the village was winding and rocky; we had trimmed the overhanging branches, but Terrans are much taller than Calliur, and their clothing catches on twigs. They are not constructed for walking through our forests. The Terran struck his head on low-hanging branches several times, and each time I offered false condolences, but did not offer guidance. Finally he switched on a blinding white light. It was then my turn to stumble, but he did not notice.

We should be accustomed to having our feelings ignored; before the Terran "liberation" our land was occupied by the cold scaly Marsi, and long ago, before the Marsi, our masters were the Lanix, who hated us because we resembled them. At least to our most recent conquerors we are thoroughly alien, and thus less threatening. The old stories say that, in ancient times, before the coming of the Lanix we were free, but I do not always believe what the stories say.

Blinded by the light I stumbled along the path and thought of the egglings in the village. Their young eyes were still sensitive. "Begging your pardon, gracious sir, but we are approaching the village and I fear for the children's sight."

The Terran stopped. "Why?"

"The light, gracious sir and governor. We are unused to such brilliance." I rubbed my eyes.

"Oh," he said, "I'm sorry. Why didn't you say something earlier?" He flicked a switch and the light turned red. "Is that better?"

I could see again. "Thank you, sir, it is an improvement. But are you able to see?"

"Well enough. By the way, my name's Hopper O'Rourke, not 'sir.' I never did hold with calling anyone 'sir'; I don't see why you should have to."

"Whatever you say, Mr. O'Rourke, sir." His manner was too friendly, and I was suspicious. We walked on.

"Well?" he said.

"Well, what, sir?"

"What's your name? Do I have to stick with 'hey, you'?"

"If it makes a difference, I am Leader Inona." Listening to myself I feared I might sound impolite, so I added, "Thank you for asking, sir, though I would of course answer to whatever you called me. Most Terrans call us all 'Calli'; it is an interchangeable name and requires no effort to remember." No, I was sounding arrogant again. I decided on silence. We were almost at the village, and I did not wish to anger him; he could order us moved to even more barren lands, away from the Before-Place, or he could cut our food ration—he might even forbid the Festival. It had been done before. As Leader I must cultivate discretion.

We left the forest and entered the clearing where the huts—made, these days, from discarded Terran refuse and packing crates—stood clustered, casting complex shadows. All three moons had risen, and there was enough light for even a Terran to see. The air was pungent with tabris root, gathered for the Festival and for export. The people were sitting in a dark quiet semicircle. Before them sat the oldest surviving Leaders.

The four Elders rose, bowed in our general direction—to the Terran or to me? They left it carefully ambiguous—and sat again. The Terran bowed in return and stood, uncertain. I gestured; an eggling ran forward and placed a leather pillow on the ground.

"Please be seated," I said. Stiff and awkward, the Terran sat on the pillow; I joined my people on the dirt. "Welcome to our village. I, as you know, am the Leader. These are the four Elders, and the people. Since some of us do not speak Terran, I will translate for you."

"Tell them I'm Hopper O'Rourke," he said, "and I've just been appointed governor of Calliur."

"*Kisa la-no-funa* O'Rourke," I began. The villagers twitched their ears and slapped the ground. I stopped. "Hopper *does* mean 'he-who-leaps,' does it not?"

"It's a nickname. My real name's Martin, and I hate it."

"Oh," I said. To change a name! Who would think of it?

"Tell them I'd like to know if they have any complaints about the way things have been run," the governor said.

"Complaints?" I was uncertain.

"You know, is there anything you don't like about the way you've been governed? I suppose there *must* be." I clicked my tongue in astonishment. *They must have resorted to sending us the bewildered and unfortunate,* I thought. But I translated his message.

There were, of course, no complaints. I could see the glitter of widened eyes and the faint skin-sheen of fear, even on the Elders. To complain requires trust and an assumption of good faith. The Terrans had earned neither.

The ceremonies concluded with one of the egglings presenting a flower to the governor and crawling backward from his presence. The Terran seemed offended. I decided to guide him back to the base; it could be dangerous for him to be out alone, as he seemed to lack the self-protective instinct.

The two brightest moons had set, and the night was dim and comfortable as we walked back to the Terran base. O'Rourke, used to a warmer climate, shivered. "Somehow I didn't think it would be so cold."

"It's not. Wait until winter. Of course we belong here, so we're used to it." I hoped my sarcasm hadn't been noticed. Evidently it had not, for he went on:

"There are a lot of things I never knew about Calliur. Oh, they briefed me on the geography, and the importance of the tabris crop, and the history of Terran occupation—but they didn't mention your compound, or the no-hunting regulation.

How do you people live? You're meat eaters, aren't you?"

"You trade us synthetic food for tabris," I said. "You decided hunting used up our valuable energy and required weapons." I had never hunted, but I remembered the old stories of the chase.

O'Rourke sounded surprised: "You let them get away with it?" I flattened my ears. He continued: "All they have to do is cut off your food supplies and you're helpless. You could starve."

"Eventually," I agreed. He did not know of the secret food stores; to build them up we had been starving ourselves for years.

"And they keep telling me how stupid and lazy you are. You *can't* be stupid; Standard Terran isn't *that* easy, especially if you don't know any of the old national tongues. And I don't know anyone who speaks your language. It must be a bitch learning a totally alien speech."

"There is a pit here. Take care." I led him around it in the darkness.

"You don't say much, do you, Inona?"

"What do you wish me to say? Welcome to Calliur. Best wishes for your term as governor. May you be healthy and prosperous. May your children be strong, and may your ancestors rest quietly."

He stopped on the path and waited until I faced him. He towered above me, his flat face gleaming white in the darkness, the smell of his clothing and skin strong and alien. "I know you don't like me," he said quietly enough. His tone was angry. "You know why I came to this God-forsaken place? You think I wanted to be governor of Calliur? My father wanted me to have a government job; I tested so low in aptitude they sent me here. It's a governorship, anyway; keeps the old man happy and keeps me out from underfoot. This is the dead-end road, the bureaucrat's burying ground!" He slapped a branch out of the way. The wood cracked, and the tree limb hung broken and useless.

I gritted my teeth, hoping he would not hear; it was a very rude gesture. "My condolences on having to govern what was once ours," I said. "The Terrans have taken such pains to hold it, I was not aware that it was less than a prize."

"If we didn't hold it the Marsi would," he said. "Would you prefer that?"

I flattened my ears. "There is little difference. Perhaps it is easier for us to serve warm-blooded masters, but you are still masters."

He laughed. "So you're the Leader. How in hell did they pick you? By heredity? It wasn't for diplomacy, I know."

"At the last Testing the Elders judged me the most alert, the one best able to see the patterns in things, the one with the quickest mind—so I became Leader. It is very simple."

"What's your term of office?" O'Rourke said.

"I serve until challenged. If one is found who is more intelligent than I, then I step down. If I reach old age I will become an Elder."

"They ought to require a little tact, too," O'Rourke said. "Of course, I was never strong on that myself."

We reached the Terran base, stark and massive in the center of a burned-out clearing. The floodlights atop the hard gray walls were blinding, and I could see the shadows of armed guards. I was afraid, but surely they would not shoot at me while I escorted O'Rourke. I walked him to the gate and hurried back to the shadows.

Later that night the Elders and I met to discuss the new governor. "I think he is incompetent," I said.

"Best to ask for more food, then," said one Elder, "while

we still can, and before he is removed."

"His relatives are powerful," I said, "or so he told me. He may not be removed for some time."

"What have relatives to do with positions of power?" It was the greatest Elder speaking. His face was scarred and the ninth finger of each hand was missing; he had been Leader during the days of the Marsi, but rarely spoke of his experiences.

"It is, I believe, a Terran custom," I said, "to judge at least partly by family."

"Strange," another Elder said. "And they continue this custom when it results in incompetence?"

"We should be grateful," I said. "This one will be easier to deal with."

I was sitting by the water gathering stones and collecting my thoughts for the Festival; I was also singing, so I did not hear footsteps until O'Rourke was almost beside me. Then I jumped, dropped the stones, and forgot my thoughts. "What are you doing here?" He must be spying. How clever, to pretend friendship and then steal into the village. But why come himself? Why not send one of his guards?

"I just thought I'd come out and see how things are going," he said. "I am the governor, after all. I ought to keep up on things." He crouched and ran his stubby fingers through the sand.

His assistants must be giving him trouble. "Things are going well," I said. I bent to my task again.

"What are you doing?"

I rose and bowed. "I am collecting stones for the Festival, Governor-sir," I said. "That is, if we have your permission to hold it."

He frowned. "Permission? Festival? Why do you need my permission?"

"Some governors disapprove of our savage ways," I said. "Especially since during the Festival we remember who we are and what we have suffered." Why did he always make me say things like that? I should resign. My mind could not be as sharp as it was supposed to be.

I pointed to the pile of stones I had dropped. "At the Festival we build cairns, adding one stone for each family member who has died at the hands of invaders. Some of the cairns are amazingly large."

O'Rourke picked up a stone. I took it from his hand, threw it far out into the water, and selected another. "That was for my mother, Ilor," I said. "She was killed in the last Rebellion."

"I'm sorry," O'Rourke said. "I didn't come to interfere with you. But I had nothing to do—my staff is so efficient, I mean —and I was wondering if you'd teach me your language."

I stared at him. This one, who had touched and profaned the memory of my mother—this one wished to learn our language? "Why?"

He shrugged. "Is it very difficult? I'd like to try."

I laughed. "You ask me if my own language is difficult? How should I know? It is different from yours, of course. But I was able to learn yours. Never has a Terran learned Calliur."

"Have any tried?"

"Not to my knowledge. Perhaps they tried and were unable. I do not know. But why should I teach you?" I moved my family stones out of his reach.

"You are the Leader, and I want to learn. I thought teaching was one of your duties."

Trapped, I looked out over the water. "You have been studying our ways. Who told you my duties? But you are not one of my people. I have no obligation to you."

He rose. "I understand. Teaching your language to a for-
eigner is too difficult and time consuming," he said. "You have
to really understand a subject before you can explain it. And,
of course, you people are all illiterate." He turned and walked
up the beach. I followed him.

"Come back after the Festival," I said. "In two days. I am
busy now." *Illiterate! The fool!* But he was nearly right.

The night of the Festival came, and the three moons rose
full and bright. We gathered near the *tials* with our family
stones and listened to the pastspeakers telling of how Brishina
fought the Lanix on their first landing and won—though why,
then, was he dead, and why had the Lanix conquered us, I
wondered—and how even the egglings had joined in the Marsi
Massacre, and had fought valiantly until overwhelmed, so
that the Marsi commander was ashamed—not that I believed
that for a moment. In all the other tales the Marsi had no
shame. Then they told how my own mother, Ilor, had killed
twenty Terrans with nothing but a spear, before she was shot.
I had been very young when she died, and I did not remember
her, so I listened to everything the pastspeakers said.

The stories were finished. I rose, carrying my stones, and
said to the people, "How long will we endure this? How long,
before we rise again?" It was a ceremonial question, and
meant little. I built my cairn, naming each stone: Ilor, Santin,
Brishina. The Elders followed me, and then the young male
Suva led the people. I watched him, slim and strong in the
moonlight, and realized he would probably succeed me.

When the commemorative ceremony was over it was time
for tabris root, dancing, and love making on the *tials* in the
moonlight, to honor our dead. We were all dazed with tabris,
but among the many who joined with me I recognized Suva.

Toward morning there was talk of rushing the Terran base, but such talk was common in the closing hours of the Festival, and nothing ever happened. When the sun rose we went back to our huts, to sleep, exhausted, through the day.

It was always talk, not action. I was sitting by the water, weighing the merit of a well-planned sober rebellion, when O'Rourke arrived. I rose, trying not to look guilty.

"How was the Festival?" he said. Did he know what I was thinking?

"We honored our dead in suitable fashion. So you have come to learn Calliur?" I did not want to speak of the Festival. He must know it made us think of rebellion; the former governors had been wise to forbid it, and O'Rourke was a fool. "I will start with simple words," I said, pointing to the first thing I saw. "*Tial.*"

"What's that?"

"A *tial*. A mass ancestral grave."

"What's two of them?"

"*Tal.*"

He shook his head. "And three?"

"*Talona.*"

"You mean you have a different case of noun for each number?"

"Sometimes. You have a different way of thinking. No doubt that is why we remain technologically backward, despite centuries of benevolent occupation." I was touchy. The Terran system of describing quantity remained a mystery.

O'Rourke ignored me and pointed to a rock. "What's that?"

"*Nar.*"

"And two of them?"

"*Nar.* It's an exception."

"Oh," said O'Rourke, and switched on a recorder. "The pronunciation is odd. Mind if I record you?"

"Not at all. I don't think you'll keep my soul in the box. And the pronunciation makes a difference."

"Na-ar."

I twitched my ears. "No, the way you said it means *sky*. It's the timing, and a falling tone." I repeated the word. This was, in a way, entertaining. I remembered my own struggles to conquer Terran prepositions, and my failure with the numerical system. Perhaps he would be shamed. I flipped a stone into the water. "*Nari*. One stone, in water."

"I thought stones had no number?"

"Well, when they're in the water they are active. It's an exception to the exception." I twitched my ears again.

He came every day, and stayed long—luckily my duties as Leader were not time consuming, or I would have had little opportunity for rest or contemplation. His progress was painfully slow. I had learned his language much faster, but for some reason he kept trying, and finally I found myself willing him to succeed.

"I don't know why you never evolved abstract numbers." O'Rourke had been making mistakes, and was on the defensive.

"We have numbers, but we don't abstract them. We talk about three articles. Your concept of *three* does not exist."

"Of course it does."

"Then show me a *three*."

O'Rourke looked around and gave up. "All right, but it's a useful tool."

"It depends," I said, "on what you consider useful. To a lowly primitive such as I, obviously only concrete situations can be real."

"Inona," O'Rourke said, "I know you don't have any reason to like me. I understand your feelings—"

"I doubt that," I said.

"Well, doubt it, then. I don't care. But have I ever given you reason to personally dislike me? On purpose—not by doing something I didn't understand, like the bright light or touching your mother's stone?"

I was surprised he remembered. They rarely did. Only their own feelings mattered. "No."

"Well," he said, "I know I said some bad things at first, and they were true, the way I saw them, but it's peaceful here, even if it *is* cold. I never wanted to be a governor anyway. I wanted to stay in school."

"Is that possible?" I said. Nowadays our egglings were taught simple housebreaking, manners, and rudimentary language; anything else they picked up later. We needed hands for the tabris gathering.

"It is more than possible. There is more than anyone could ever learn, no matter how long his lifetime. And things keep changing. But I didn't have any money of my own, and my father was ashamed of what he called a 'professional student' —he was determined I'd *be* somebody. So he got me a post as planetary governor. Big deal." He laughed. "I know, it's your world and you love it. You've never seen another, and God knows you've had a hard enough time trying to hang onto it —there aren't many of you left—but compared to all the planets out there this one isn't much. There are places where it's warm, and where the plants are green, not blue, and the sun is yellow—Earth, for instance."

I was too interested to be offended. Besides, he was entitled to his opinion. "I am told that most stars have planets," I said. "At night I see many of them."

"There are more than you could count," he said. "Many

more than you can see." We were still sitting by the water; he picked up a stone, paused, and said, "May I?" I looked at him, puzzled for a moment, then understood what he meant.

"Of course," I said. "It isn't anyone today." He smiled and pitched it into the water. "Once active stone," he said.

It was then I realized we'd been speaking almost pure Calliur.

It was late afternoon; the Elders and I sat in the village clearing. The huts cast long, discouraged-looking shadows. The days were growing colder, and there were rumors of trouble.

"It is time, now," an Elder said. "The Terran leader is weak, and there is dissension in the base. My egglings' egglings have heard the guards talking behind the wall; they say O'Rourke is mad, and they want to rid themselves of him."

"And my informants," said a second Elder, "tell me that if he is sent away there will be more repression. There is disagreement about the new food allotments—some of the clerks are certain we are hoarding—and the Festival—"

"Why do they want us anyhow?" the greatest Elder said. His teeth were blunt with age, but in his scarred face his snarl was still frightening.

"Tabris. They use it for medicine. And if the Terrans did not hold our planet, the Marsi would—and with it they would control our entire star system. Or so I have been told." The Elders bared their teeth at me; I realized I had said something wrong.

"You were told this by O'Rourke the Mad," the greatest Elder said. "He who learns our language, to spy on us. He whom you are teaching, while neglecting your other duties."

"I do not think he wants to spy on us," I said. "Nor do I think he has the ability. He has good will, but poor judgment."

"Like yourself," the greatest Elder said. "You have shown

exceedingly poor judgment. You have trusted a conqueror. Now that he has our speech, who knows what may happen? You should have asked our counsel."

"I am Leader," I said, "and I ask for counsel when I need it." I was angry; I should not have answered him thus. He looked at his mutilated hands.

"You trusted a conqueror," he said. "You may be Leader no longer. There is Suva. He should be examined for leadership, do you not agree?" He turned to the others; they looked at me with hatred.

I already knew the results of the testing. Suva was capable, and the Elders were against me. There was nothing for me to do but leave. I walked from the village in silence and went to the Before-Place.

It had been a long time since I had last been to the ruins. The wind-sharpened stones cast intricate shadows on the ground, and the spiral carvings were weathered and aged. Groundcover flourished in the old courtyard, and the roof of the building had caved in, leaving the walls to whistle lonely in the wind. I sat on the remnants of a carved bench and looked at the ruined portal.

LIGHT OF FOREVER. Could I really read the tracings, or was I working by rote memory? I no longer knew. So few things were written any more. Messages were passed by word of mouth. What history did we have that the pastspeakers could not relate and embellish better than if it were written?

I circled the building looking for the other inscriptions. HOME OF JUSTICE, said one. I recognized the whorls and spirals. ENDURE, the other said. Whatever was to have endured had crumbled; only the word remained.

The wind sang coldly through the gray stones, and the groundcover rustled dry and dead. I knelt, cleared away some rubble, and tried to write my name. INONA—surely that was it, that combination of wavy lines and circles? I looked up. No, that was part of an inscription. I tried again. INONA. I had to remember.

And then I thought, even if I could write my name, could I write anything else? What did the squiggles and spirals mean? Which of them were connected to form words? How did we translate the sound to the symbol? I could not remember.

I traced meaningless designs in the dust, then walked slowly back to the village. Suva sat with the Elders, as new Leader. He looked ashamed, yet triumphant. I joined in the polite handclapping, then went to my miserable hut and stared at the sagging plywood ceiling.

I did not eat even the small amount we rationed ourselves, and my eggs died within me. Birthing them was painful and unrewarding. I gave them simple names and wondered if they could be considered family members killed in battle, but then I decided they could not, and I buried them in the *tial* of the never-lived.

People shunned me even more than customary with a deposed Leader, for had I not consorted with the enemy, a Terran? I myself could not imagine why I had done so, but O'Rourke was stupid, and yet well-meaning. He had, I realized, always managed to make me angry, usually to his own ends. Perhaps he was not so stupid after all.

I was sitting in my favorite spot near the water—alone, of course—when he found me. "I tried to visit you several times," he said, "but they told me you were ill and could see no one." He looked at me. "You are thinner, and pale." He, too, had lost flesh, and his bright hair was dull and old-looking.

I wrapped my arms around myself. The wind felt cold, and

my winter fur was sparse. "I lost my eggs. You look more aged yourself. How have things been?"

He sat and rested his head on his knees. "I don't know. I think they're trying to get rid of me—I'm sure of it—but so far they've tried through official channels. I monitored a broadcast. My father's too important. They'll never get rid of me that way."

"Well, then, what can they do?" I said.

He picked up a stone and hefted it. "Kill me, I suppose." He tossed it out into the water.

I was shocked. "Kill you, to get you out of office? Why can they not depose you? I myself have been deposed, but none thought of killing me."

He looked up. "I didn't know that," he said. "What happened? Was it because you were sick?"

"No," I said, and would answer no further questions. I could not tell him that the Elders planned rebellion—that would be treason—and if I told him his friendship had been my downfall . . . I realized, suddenly, that his feelings meant something. "Politics, on a very minor, savage scale, of course."

We sat and watched the waves wash against the shore. There was frost on the beach.

When the Terrans cut our food supplies below the survival minimum I anticipated trouble; when, in O'Rourke's name, they forbade the Festival, I understood. I had not seen O'Rourke for some time. There were more guards now at the Terran base, and the lights were bright enough to keep even our informers away.

No one would confide in me, but I could tell a rebellion was planned. So, of course, could the Terrans; it was obvious. They could see us cutting trees for spears, making catapults, training late into the night; they could sense the excitement that kept the new Leader and the Elders from protesting the food shortage—thus betraying the existence of the hoard—it was painfully obvious. Or had I come to think like a Terran?

But even I was unprepared for what they would do. On the Festival night, when we sat sullen and quiet, forbidden even to approach the *tials* or to gather in groups, the Terrans went in force to the Before-Place and rayed the ruins. We could see the glow from the village; by the time we arrived the stone walls had melted like ice, and fires were raging in the ground-cover. It was too late to save the building, and we could not control the fires. The Terrans retreated to their base; furious, we pursued them. I was afraid, but there was no reasoning with the crowd, and I was swept along.

The glaring lights were turned off, and the moonlight revealed the gate standing open. I was sure, then, of a trap, but could do nothing; brandishing spears and shouting, we swept through the gate.

None of us had ever seen the inside of the Terran compound; we did not know what to expect. There was little damage we could do. Inside the wall was an open space, and then a fortresslike building with smooth metal sides.

We stood, uncertain, when a door opened in the wall and O'Rourke emerged. I am sure he was pushed; I saw him stumble, recover, and turn angrily, only to face a closed door. The crowd advanced. O'Rourke turned and beat on the wall, calling for assistance; he was ignored. He turned back to us.

"I had nothing to do with it," he said, "believe me." He spoke Calliur, but no one listened. "It's a plot; you're being used. They want to get rid of me, and they can't." A spear flew past his head and clanged against metal. I darted to the front of the crowd, trying to reach him.

"Let me by," I said. I was ignored, shoved, trampled. I seized a spear and forced my way through.

Silent now, the crowd drew closer to O'Rourke. He stopped

talking and looked at them. He stood before the wall, arms hanging limp at his sides. He started to say something, then stopped.

I pushed to the front of the crowd and stood before him. "He's right," I said. "We're being used. Why do you think they destroyed the Before-Place, forbade the Festival, cut the food rations? They *want* a rebellion."

The greatest Elder stood at the front of the crowd; wordless, he pulled me aside and struck at O'Rourke. It was a signal; Suva and the others thrust spears into the Terran, and he fell. The pastspeakers were right about one thing: their blood is red. O'Rourke's last expression was one of amazement, and pain.

The lights came on and armed guards poured into the courtyard, shooting. We fled.

There were, of course, severe reprisals; the Terrans had to show disapproval of the rebellion. There were no Festivals for three years; food rationing wiped out our hoard, and our village was burned to the ground. Suva and the Elders were executed; we buried them with the honored dead. My being spared did nothing to increase my popularity. The new governor visited our village once, under heavy guard, and then had no further contact with us. We harvested tabris, chose a new leader, and life went on.

Time eventually allayed suspicion, and it was acknowledged that I had not betrayed the rebellion; I was again accepted. I was by then the oldest surviving Leader, so I became an Elder, though I rarely offered advice.

Already the pastspeakers were telling of the glorious revolution, and how we had shown great bravery in fighting the Terrans. They made O'Rourke to be a tyrant, and his killing an act of valor. I said nothing, and waited.

In time the Festival was again permitted, and I collected

my stones and built my cairn next to the *tial*. Loudly, clearly I named my family's dead: Brishina, Santin, Ilor, and O'Rourke.

The dead whisper angrily if I approach the *tial*, and I am no longer welcome in the village, so I spend most of my time in the ruins of the Before-Place. I wonder what the building might have been. It is winter again, and the wind is cold; it whistles over the scars left by the heat rays. The inscriptions are gone, and we have no more written words. I think of how the pastspeakers have made the rebellions great and glorious things, and of how the egglings believe them. I wish there were some way to record true history. I would gladly learn to write Terran, if any man would be fool enough to teach me.

Do You Know Dave Wenzel?

Fritz Leiber

We come now to a very basic question: Exactly what is an alien? Fritz Leiber suggests that sometimes we ourselves may harbor alien creatures within us—and we may not always be able to keep our private aliens hidden.

Fritz Leiber is one of the great writers of science fiction and fantasy, author of such Hugo-winning novels as The Big Time *and* The Wanderer.

When Don Senior said, "There's the bell," and pushed back his chair, Wendy had just upset her bowl, John's hand was creeping across the edge of his plate to join forces with his spoon, and Don Junior had begun to kick the table leg as he gazed into space at an invisible adventure comic.

Katherine spared Don Senior a glance from the exacting task of getting the top layer of mashed carrots back into the bowl while holding off Wendy's jumpy little paws. "I didn't even hear it," she said.

"I'll answer it," Don Senior told her.

Three minutes later Wendy's trancelike spoon-to-mouth routine was operating satisfactorily, John's hand had made a strategic withdrawal, and the rest of the carrots had been wiped up. Don Junior had quietly gone to the window and was standing with his head poked between the heavy rose drapes looking out across the dark lawn—perhaps at more of the invisible adventure, Katherine thought. She watched him fondly. *Little boys are so at the mercy of their dreams. When the "call" comes, they have to answer it. Girls are different.*

Don seemed rather thoughtful when he came back to the table. Suddenly like Don Junior, it occurred to Katherine.

"Who was it, dear?"

He looked at her for a moment, oddly, before replying.

"An old college friend."

"Didn't you invite him in?"

He shook his head, glancing at the children. "He's gone down in the world a long way," he said softly. "Really pretty disreputable."

Katherine leaned forward on her elbows. "Still, if he was once a friend—"

"I'm afraid you wouldn't like him," he said decisively, yet it seemed to Katherine with a shade of wistfulness.

"Did I ever meet him?" she asked.

"No. His name's Dave Wenzel."

"Did he want to borrow money?"

Don seemed not to hear that question. Then, "Money? Oh no!"

"But what did he want to see you about?"

Don didn't answer. He sat frowning.

The children had stopped eating. Don Junior turned from the window. The drapes dropped together behind him.

"Did he go away, Dad?" Don Junior asked.

"Of course."

"But I didn't see him go."

It was quiet for several moments. Then Don Senior said, "He must have cut around the other side of the house."

"How strange," Katherine said. Then, smiling quickly at the children, she asked, "Have you ever seen him since college, Don?"

"Not since the day I graduated."

"Let's see, how long is that?" She made a face of dismay, mockingly. "Oh Lord, it's getting to be a long time. Fourteen, fifteen years. And this is the same month."

Again her husband looked at her intently. "As it happens," he said, "it's exactly the same day."

When Katherine dropped in at her husband's office the next morning, she was thinking about the mysterious Mr. Wenzel. Not because the incident had stuck in her mind particularly, but because it had been recalled by a chance meeting on the train coming up to town, with another college friend of her husband.

Katherine felt good. It is pleasant to meet an old beau and find that you still attract him and yet have the reassuring knowledge that all the painful and exciting uncertainties of youth are done with.

How lucky I am to have Don, she thought. *Other wives have to worry about women (I wonder how Carleton Hare's wife makes out?) and failure (Is Mr. Wenzel married?) and moods and restlessness and a kind of little-boy rebelliousness against the business of living. But Don is different. So handsome, yet so true. So romantic, yet so regular. He has a quiet heart.*

She greeted the secretary. "Is Mr. McKenzie busy?"

"He has someone with him now. A Mr. Wenzel, I think."

Katherine did not try to conceal her curiosity. "Oh, tell me about him, would you? What does he look like?"

"I really don't know," Miss Korshak said, smiling. "Mr. McKenzie told me there would be a Mr. Wenzel to see him, and I think he came in a few minutes ago, while I was away from the desk. I know Mr. McKenzie has a visitor now, because I heard him talking to someone. Shall I ring your husband, Mrs. McKenzie?"

"No, I'll wait a while." Katherine sat down and pulled off her gloves.

A few minutes later Miss Korshak picked up some papers and went off. Katherine wandered to the door of her husband's office. She could hear his voice every now and then, but she couldn't make out what he was saying. The panel of frosted glass showed only vague masses of light and shadow. She felt a sudden touch of uneasiness. She lifted her hand, which was dusted with freckles almost the same shade as her hair, and knocked.

All sound from beyond the door ceased. Then there were footsteps and the door opened.

Don looked at her blankly for a moment. Then he kissed her.

She went ahead of him into the gray-carpeted office.

"But where is Mr. Wenzel?" she asked, turning to him with a gesture of half-playful amazement.

"He just happened to be finished," Don said lightly, "so he left by the hall door."

"He must be an unusually shy person—and very quiet,"
Katherine said. "Don, did you arrange with him last night to
come and see you here?"

"In a way."

"What is he after, Don?"

Her husband hesitated. "I suppose you could describe him
as a kind of crank."

"Does he want you to publish some impossible article in
your magazine?"

"No, not exactly." Don grimaced and waved a hand as if in
mild exasperation. "Oh, you know the type, dear. The old college friend who's a failure and who wants to talk over old
times. The sort of chap who gets a morbid pleasure out of
dwelling on old ideas and reviving old feelings. Just a born
botherer." And he quickly went on to ask her about her shop-
ping, and she mentioned running into Carleton Hare, and
there was no more talk of Dave Wenzel.

But when Katherine got home later that afternoon after
picking up the children at Aunt Martha's, she found that Don
had called to say not to wait dinner. When he finally did get
in he looked worried. As soon as the children were asleep, Don
and Katherine settled themselves in the living room in front
of the fireplace. Don made a fire, and the sharp odor of burning hardwood mingled with the scent of freesias set in a dull
blue bowl on the mantelpiece under the Monet.

As soon as the flames were leaping, Katherine asked seriously, "Don, what is this thing about Dave Wenzel?"

He started to make light of the question, but she interrupted, "No, really, Don. Ever since you came back from
the door last night, you've had something on your mind. And
it isn't at all like you to turn away old friends or shoo them
out of your office, even if they have become a bit seedy. What
is it, Don?"

"It's nothing to worry about, really."

"I'm not worried, Don. I'm just curious." She hesitated. "And maybe a bit shuddery."

"Shuddery?"

"I have an eerie feeling about Wenzel, perhaps because of the way he disappeared so quietly both times, and then—oh, I don't know, but I do want to know about him, Don."

He looked at the fire for a while and its flames brought orange tints to his skin. Then he turned to her with a shame-faced smile and said, "Oh, I don't mind telling you about it. Only it's pretty silly. And it makes me look silly, too."

"Good," she said with a laugh, turning toward him on the couch and drawing her feet under her. "I've always wanted to hear something silly about you, Don."

"I don't know," he said. "You might even find it a little disgusting. And very small-boy. You know, swearing oaths and all that."

She had a flash of inspiration. "You mean the business of it being fifteen years, to the exact day?"

He nodded. "Yes, that was part of it. There was some sort of agreement between us. A compact."

"Oh good, a mystery," she said with lightly mocked childishness, not feeling as secure as she pretended.

He paused. He reached along the couch and took her hand. "You must remember," he said, squeezing it, "that the Don McKenzie I'm going to tell you about is not the Don McKenzie you know now, not even the one you married. He's a different Don, younger, much less experienced, rather shy and gauche, lonely, a great dreamer, with a lot of mistaken ideas about life and a lot of crazy notions . . . of all sorts."

"I'll remember," she said, returning the pressure of his fingers. "And Dave Wenzel, how am I to picture him?"

"About my age, of course. But with a thinner face and deep-sunk eyes. He was my special friend." He frowned. "You know, you have your ordinary friends in college, the ones you room with, play tennis, go on dates. They're generally solid and reliable, your kind. But then there's a special friend, and oddly enough he's not so apt to be solid and reliable."

Again he frowned. "I don't know why, but he's apt to be a rather disreputable character, someone you're a bit ashamed of and wouldn't want your parents to meet.

"But he's more important to you than anyone, because he shares your crazier dreams and impulses. In fact, you're probably attracted to him in the first place because you feel he possesses those dreams and impulses even more strongly than you do."

"I think I understand," Katherine said wisely, not altogether certain that she did. She heard Don Junior call in his sleep and she listened a moment and looked attentively at her husband. *How extraordinarily bright his eyes are,* she thought.

"Dave and I would have long bull sessions in my room and we'd go for long walks at night, all over the campus, down by the lake front, and through the slum districts. And always the idea between us was to keep alive a wonderful, glamorous dream. Sometimes we'd talk about the books we liked and the weirder things we'd seen. Sometimes we'd make up crazy experiences and tell them to each other as if they were true. But mostly we'd talk about our ambitions, the amazing, outrageous things we were going to do someday."

"And they were—?"

He got up and began to pace restlessly. "That's where it begins to get so silly," he said. "We were going to be great scholars and at the same time we were going to tramp all over the world and have all sorts of adventures."

How like Don Junior, she thought. *But Don Junior's so much younger. When he goes to college, will he still . . . ?*

"We were going to experience danger and excitement in every form. I guess we were going to be a couple of Casanovas, too."

Her humorous "Hmf!" was lost as he hurried on, and despite herself, his words began to stir her imagination. "We were going to do miraculous things with our minds, like a mystic does. Telepathy. Clairvoyance. We were going to take drugs. We were going to find out some great secret that's been hidden ever since the world began. I think if Dave said, 'We'll go to the moon, Don,' I'd have believed him."

He came to a stop in front of the fire. Slitting his eyes, he said slowly, as if summing up, "We were like knights preparing to search for some modern, unknown, and rather dubious grail. And someday in the course of our adventuring we were going to come face to face with the reality behind life and death and time and all those other big ideas."

For a moment, for just a moment, Katherine seemed to feel the spinning world under her and, as if the walls and ceiling had faded, to see her husband's big-shouldered body jutting up against a background of black space and stars.

She thought, *Never before has he seemed so wonderful. And never so frightening.*

He shook his finger at her, almost angrily, she felt. "And then one night, one terrible night before I graduated, we suddenly saw just how miserably weak we were, how utterly impossible of realizing the tiniest of our ambitions. There we were, quite floored by all the minor problems of money and jobs and independence and sex, and dreaming of the sky! We realized that we'd have to establish ourselves in the world, learn how to deal with people, become seasoned men of action, solve all the minor problems, before we could ever tackle the big quest. We gave ourselves fifteen years to bring all those small things under control. Then we were to meet and get going."

Katherine didn't know it was going to happen, but she suddenly started to laugh, almost hysterically. "Excuse me, dear," she managed to say after a moment, noting Don's puzzled expression, "but you and your friend did so get the cart before the horse! Back then you had a chance for some adventure, at least you were free. But you had to go and pick on the time when you'd be most tied down." And she started to laugh again.

For an instant Don looked hurt, then he began to laugh with her. "Of course, dear, I understand all that now, and it seems the most ridiculous thing in the world to me. When I opened the door last night and saw Dave standing there expectantly in a sleazy coat, with a lot less hair than I remembered, I was completely dumbfounded. Of course I'd forgotten about our compact years ago, long before you and I were married."

She started to laugh again. "And so I was one of your minor problems, Don?" she asked teasingly.

"Of course not, dear!" He pulled her up from the couch and hugged her boisterously. Katherine quickly closed her mind to the thought *He's changed since I laughed—he's shut something up inside him,* and welcomed the sense of security that flooded back into her at his embrace.

When they were settled again, she said, "Your friend must have been joking when he came around last night. There are people who will wait years for a laugh."

"No, he was actually quite serious."

"I can't believe it. Incidentally, just how well has he done at fulfilling of his end of the bargain—I mean, establishing himself in the world?"

"Not well at all. In fact, so badly that, as I say, I didn't want him in the house last night."

"Then I'll bet it's the financial backing for this quest that he's thinking about."

"No, I honestly don't think he's looking for money."

Katherine leaned toward him. She was suddenly moved by the old impulse to measure every danger, however slight. "Tell you what, Don. You get your friend to spruce up a bit and we'll invite him to dinner. Maybe arrange a couple of parties. I'll bet that if he met some women it would make all the difference."

"Oh no, that's out of the question," Don said sharply. "He isn't that sort of person at all. It wouldn't work."

"Very well," Katherine said, shrugging. "But in that case how are you going to get rid of him?"

"Oh, that'll be easy," Don said.

"How did he take it when you refused?"

"Rather hard," Don admitted.

"I still can't believe he was serious."

Don shook his head. "You don't know Dave."

Katherine caught hold of his hand. "Tell me one thing," she said. "How seriously, how really seriously, did you take this . . . compact, when you made it?"

He looked at the fire before he said, "I told you I was a different Don McKenzie then."

"Don," she said, and her voice dropped a little, "is there anything dangerous about this? Is Dave altogether honorable —or sane? Are you going to have any trouble getting rid of him?"

"Of course not, dear! I tell you it's all done with." He caught her in his arms. But for a moment Katherine felt that his voice, though hearty, lacked the note of complete certainty.

And during the next few days she had reason to think that her momentary feeling had been right. Don stayed late at the office a little more often than usual, and twice when she called him during the day, he was out and Miss Korshak didn't know where to locate him. His explanations, given casually, were always very convincing, but he didn't look well and he'd acquired a nervous manner. At home he began to answer the phone ahead of her, and one or two of the conversations he held over it were cryptic.

Even the children, Katherine felt, had caught something of the uneasiness.

She found herself studying Don Junior rather closely, looking for traits that might increase her understanding of his father. She went over in her mind what she knew of Don Senior's childhood and was bothered at how little there was. (*But isn't that true of many city childhoods?* she asked herself.) Just a good, conscientious boy, brought up mostly by two rather stuffy yet emotional aunts. The only escapade she remembered hearing about was once when he'd stayed at a movie all afternoon and half the night.

She was up against the realization that a whole section of her husband's thoughts were locked off from her. And since this had never happened before, she was frightened. Don loved her as much as ever, she was sure of that. But something was eating at him.

Weren't success and a loving wife and children, she wondered, enough for a man? Enough in a serious way, that is, for anyone might have his frivolities, his trivial weaknesses (though actually Don had neither). Or was there something more, something beyond that? Not religion, not power, not fame, but . . .

She badly needed more people around, so when Carleton Hare called up she impulsively invited him to dinner. His wife, Carleton said, was out of town.

It was one of those evenings when Don called up at the

last minute to say he wouldn't be able to get home for dinner. (No, he couldn't make it even for Carleton—something had come up at the printer's. Awfully glad Carleton had come, though. Hoped very much to see him later in the evening, but might be very late—don't wait up.)

After the children were shepherded off and Katherine and Carleton had paraded rather formally into the living room, she asked, "Did you know a college friend of Don's named Dave Wenzel?"

Katherine got the impression that her question had thrown Carleton off some very different line of conversation he had been plotting in his mind. "No, I didn't," he said a little huffily. "Name's a bit familiar, but I don't think I ever met the man."

But then he seemed to reconsider. He turned toward Katherine, so that the knees of his knife-creased gray trousers were a few inches closer to hers along the couch.

"Wait a minute," he said, "Don did have an odd friend of some sort. I think his name may have been Wenzel. Don sometimes bragged about him—how brilliant this man was, what wild exciting experiences he'd had. But somehow, none of us fellows ever met him.

"I hope you won't mind my saying this," he continued with a boyish chuckle that startled Katherine a bit, it was so perfect. "But Don was rather shy and moody at college, not very successful socially and inclined to be put out about it. Some of us even thought this friend of his—yes, I'm sure the name was Wenzel—was just an imaginary person he'd cooked up in his mind to impress us with."

"You did?" Katherine asked.

"Oh yes. Once we insisted on his bringing this Wenzel around to a party. He agreed, but then it turned out that Wenzel had left town on some mysterious and important jaunt."

"Mightn't it have been that he was ashamed of Wenzel for some reason?" Katherine asked.

"Yes, I suppose it might," Carleton agreed doubtfully. "Tell me, Kat," he went on, "how do you get along with a moody, introspective person like Don?"

"Very well."

"Are you happy?" Carleton asked, his voice a little deeper. Katherine smiled. "I think so."

Carleton's hand, moving along the couch, covered hers. "Of course you are," he said. "An intelligent, well-balanced person like yourself wouldn't be anything else but happy. But how vivid is that happiness? How often, for instance, do you realize what a completely charming woman you are? Aren't there times—not all the time, of course—when, with a simpler, more vital sort of person, you could . . ."

She shook her head, looking into his eyes with a childlike solemnity. "No, Carleton, there aren't," she said, gently withdrawing her hand from under his.

Carleton blinked, and his head, which had been moving imperceptibly toward hers, stopped with a jerk. Katherine's lips twitched and she started to talk about the children.

During the rest of the evening Carleton didn't by any means give up the attack. But he carried it on in an uninspired fashion, as if merely to comply with the tenets of male behavior. Katherine wanted to burst out laughing, he was so solemn and dogged about it, and once he caught her smiling at him rather hysterically, and he put on an injured look. She tried to pump him, rather cruelly, she felt, about Dave Wenzel and Don, but he apparently knew nothing beyond what he had told her. He left rather early. Katherine couldn't help suspecting that he was relieved to go.

She went to bed. Her somewhat sorry amusement at Carleton Hare faded. The minutes dragged on, as she waited for Don.

A voice woke her. A mumbling distant voice. She was hot with sleep and the dark walls of the bedroom pulsated painfully, as if they were inside her eyes.

At first she thought it was Don Junior. She felt her way into the hall. Then she realized that the voice was coming from downstairs. It would go on for a while, rising a bit, then it would break off several seconds before starting again. It seemed to pulsate with the darkness.

She crept downstairs barefooted. The house was dark. Dimly she could see the white rectangle of the door to Don's study. It was closed and no light showed through the cracks. Yet it was from there that the voice seemed to be coming.

"For the last time I tell you, Dave, I won't. Yes, I've gone back on my word, but I don't care. The whole thing is off."

Katherine's hand trembled on the smooth round of the stair post. It was Don's voice, but tortured, frantic, and yet terribly controlled, like she had never heard it before.

"What's a promise made by a child? Besides, the whole thing's ridiculous, impossible."

She tiptoed toward the door, step by step.

"All right then, Dave, I believe you. We could do everything you say. But I don't want to. I'm going to hold fast to my own."

Now she was crouching by the door and she still couldn't hear the answering voice in the silences. But her imagination supplied it: a whisper that had strength in it, and richness, and mockery, and a certain oily persuasiveness.

"What do I care if my life is drab and monotonous?" Her husband's voice was growing louder. "I tell you I don't want the far cities, and dark streets shimmering with danger. I don't want the gleaming nights and the burning days. I don't want space. I don't want the stars!"

Again silence, and again that suggestion of a resonant

whisper, adrip with beauty and evil.

Then, "All right, so the people I know are miserable little worms, men of cardboard and dusty, dry-mouthed puppets. I don't mind. Do you understand, I don't mind! I don't want to meet the people whose emotions are jewels, whose actions are sculptured art. I don't want to know the men like gods. I don't want my mind to meet their minds with a crash like music or the sea."

Katherine was trembling again. Her hand went up and down the door like a moth, hovering, not quite touching it.

"So my mind's small, is it? Well, let it be. Let someone else's consciousness swell and send out tentacles. I don't want the opium dreams. I don't want the more-than-opium dream. I don't care if I never glimpse the great secrets of far shores. I don't care if I die with blinders over my eyes. I don't care, do you hear, I don't care!"

Katherine swayed, as if a great wind were blowing through the door. She writhed as if each word scalded her.

"But I tell you I don't want any woman but Kat!" Her husband's voice was filled with agony. "I don't care how young and beautiful they are. I don't care if they're only twenty. Kat's enough for me. Do you hear that, Dave? Kat's enough. Dave! Stop it, Dave! Stop it!"

There was a pounding. Katherine realized she had thrown herself against the door and was beating on it. She grabbed the knob, snatched it open, and darted inside.

There was a whirling of shadows, a gasping exclamation, three pounding footsteps, a great crash of glass, a whish of leaves. Something struck her shoulder and she staggered sideways, found the wall, groped along it, pushed the light switch.

The light hurt. In it, Don's face looked peeled. He was turning back from the big picture window, now a jagged hole of darkness through which the cool night was pouring and a green twig intruded. In it, only a few daggers and corners of glass remained. A chair lay on the floor, overturned. Don stared at her as if she were a stranger.

"Did he . . . jump out?" she asked shakily, wetting her lips.

Don nodded blindly. Then a look of rage grew on his face. He started toward her, taking deliberate steps, swaying a little.

"Don!"

He stopped. Slowly recognition replaced rage. Then he suddenly grimaced with what might have been shame or agony, or both, and turned away.

She moved to him quickly, putting her arms around him. "Oh, what is it, Don?" she said. "Please, Don, let me help you."

He shrank away from her.

"Don," she said hollowly after a moment, forcing the words, "If you really want to go off with this man . . . "

His back, turned to her, writhed. "No! No!"

"But then what is it, Don? How can he make you act this way? What sort of hold does he have on you?"

He shook his head hopelessly.

"Tell me, Don, please, how can he torment you so? Oh please, Don!"

Silence.

"But what are we going to do, Don? He . . . oh he must be insane," she said, looking uneasily at the window, "to do a thing like that. Will he come back? Will he lurk around? Will he . . . oh, don't you see, Don, we can't have it like that. There are the children. Don, I think we should call the police."

He looked around quickly, his face quite calm. "Oh no, we can't do that," he said quietly. "Under no circumstances."

"But if he keeps on . . ."

"No," Don said, looking at her intently. "I'll settle the whole matter, myself, Kat. I don't want to talk about it now, but I promise you that it will be settled. And there will be no more incidents like tonight. You have my word on it." He paused. "Well, Kat?"

For a moment she met his eyes. Then, unwillingly—she had the queer feeling that it was the pressure of his stare that made her do it—she dipped her head.

During the next two weeks there were many times when she desperately wished she had insisted on bringing things to a head that night, for it marked the beginning of a reign of terror that was all the more unnerving because it could not be laid to any very definite incidents. Shadows on the lawn, small noises at the windows, the suggestion of a lurking figure, doors open that should be closed—there is nothing conclusive about such things. But they nibble at courage.

The children felt it, of that Katherine was sure. Don Junior started asking questions about witches and horrors, and he wasn't quite so brave about going upstairs at night. Sometimes she caught him looking at her or at his father in a way that made her wish she didn't have to be so untroubled and cheerful in his presence and could talk to him more freely. John came to share their bed more often in the middle of the night, and Wendy would wake whimpering.

Don's behavior was very reassuring for the first few days. He was brisk and businesslike, not moody at all, and had an unusually large supply of jokes for the children and of complimentary remarks for her—though Katherine couldn't shake the feeling that these were all carefully prepared and cost him considerable effort. But she couldn't get near him. He showed an artfulness quite unlike his ordinary self at avoiding serious discussions. The two or three times she finally blurted out some question about Dave Wenzel or his feelings, he would only frown and say quickly, "Please don't let's talk about it now. It only makes it harder for me."

She tried to think herself close to him, but when a contact between you and the man you love is broken, thoughts aren't much help. And when you feel that the love is still there, that only makes it the more baffling, for it leaves you nothing to bite against. Don was slipping away from her. He was growing dim. And there was nothing she could do to stop it.

And always the long brittle train of her thoughts would be snapped by some small but ominous incident that set her nerves quivering.

Then the reassuring aspects of Don's behavior began to fade. He became silent and preoccupied, both with her and with the children. His emotions began to show in his face—gloomy, despairing ones, they seemed. The children noticed that, too. At dinner Katherine's heart would sink when she saw Don Junior's glance lift surreptitiously from his plate to his father. And Don didn't look at all well, either. He got thinner and there were dark circles under his eyes, and his movements became fretful and nervous.

He had a habit, too, of staying near the hall when he was at home, so that it was always he who answered the door as well as the telephone.

Sometimes he'd go out late at night, saying he was restless and needed a walk. He might be home in fifteen minutes—or four hours.

Still Katherine made efforts to get through to him. But he seemed to sense what she was going to say, and the look of pain and misery on his face would choke off her question.

Finally she could stand her fear and uncertainty no longer. It was something Don Junior told her that gave her courage to act. He came home from school with a story of a man who had been standing outside the playground at recess and who had walked behind him on the way home.

That evening before dinner, she went to Don and said simply, "I am going to call the police."

He looked at her closely for several seconds and then replied in as calm a voice as hers, "Very well; I only ask you to wait until tomorrow morning."

"It's no use, Don," she said. "I've got to do it. Since you won't tell me what this cloud is that's hanging over you, I must take my own precautions. I don't know what you'll tell the police when they talk to you, but . . ."

"I'll tell them everything," he said, "tomorrow morning."

"Oh Don," she said, stiffening her face to hold back emotion, "I don't want to hurt you, but you leave me nothing else to do. I gave in to you before; I gave you time to settle the matter in your own way. I was willing to let whatever it is be a closed door, so long as it was closed, but things have only got worse. If I give in to you now, you'll ask me to give in to you again tomorrow morning. And I can't stand any more of it."

"That's not fair," he said judiciously. "I never set a date before. I am setting one now. It's a very small thing I'm asking of you, Kat. Just a few more hours in which to"—suddenly his face grew very hard—"settle this matter for once and all. Please give me those hours, Kat."

After a moment she sighed and her shoulders slumped. "Very well," she said. "Except I won't have the children in the house tonight. I'll take them to Aunt Martha's."

"That's quite all right," he said. He bowed his head to her and walked up the stairs.

Calling Aunt Martha, spinning an explanation for her, convincing the children that this was the jolliest of impromptu expeditions—these were tasks that Katherine welcomed for the momentary relief they gave. And there were a couple of moments, driving over to Martha's with the children all piled in the front seat beside her, when she felt almost carefree.

She drove home immediately, after repeating to Aunt Martha her story of a sudden invitation she and Don had gotten to a city party given by a publisher whose favor Don particularly courted. When she arrived, Don was gone.

The house had never seemed so empty, so like a trap. But as she crossed the threshold, she gave over the control of herself to that same cold will power she had depended on earlier that evening in talking to Don. She didn't wander through the house; she didn't let herself stand aimlessly for a moment. She picked up a book and sat down with it in the living room, reading the meaningless words carefully. She did not let her gaze stray occasionally toward the dark windows and doorways, though she knew that would have been normal. That was all.

At ten-thirty she put down her book, went upstairs, bathed, went down to the kitchen, heated some milk, drank it, and went up to bed.

She lay on her back, wide-eyed, motionless, almost without thoughts. Occasionally the lights of a car would sweep across the ceiling. Very rarely, for it was a still night, the leaves outside the window would whisper. She felt that for the rest of her life this sort of trance would substitute for sleep.

It must have been at least three when she heard the key grate in the lock of the front door. She did not move. She heard the door open and close, then cautious steps coming up the stairs and along the hall. A dark shape paused outside the half-open bedroom door, then went on. There was the snick of a light switch and the hall glowed dimly. A little later came the sound of running water.

Katherine got up quietly and looked into the hall. The bathroom door was open and the light was on. Don was standing in front of the wash basin, holding something wrapped in newspapers. She watched him unwrap something that flashed —a long hunting knife.

He inspected it minutely, then laid it down on the newspapers.

He took off his coat and looked it all over, particularly the sleeves. He frowned, soaped a washrag, and rubbed one of the cuffs. Likewise he inspected his trousers and shirt.

He took off his shoes and carefully rubbed them all over, including the soles, with the washrag.

He looked over his hands and bare arms inch by inch. Then he critically studied his face in the mirror, twisting it this way and that.

Katherine swayed. Her wrist knocked the wall. He jerked around, tense, on guard. She went toward him, taking short unsteady steps. "Don," she gasped out, "what have you done?"

There came over his face a look of utter tiredness and apathy. He blinked his eyes flickeringly.

"I did what you wanted me to," he said dully, not looking at her. "I got rid of Wenzel. He'll never trouble you again."

Her gasps formed the words. "No. No."

He lifted his hand toward her. "Dave Wenzel is dead, Katherine," he said very distinctly. "I have finished off Dave Wenzel forever. Do you understand me, Katherine?"

As he spoke the words, the wild tiredness seemed to drain from his eyes, to be replaced (as if he had spoken words of exorcism) by a clear steadiness that she hadn't seen in them for weeks.

But Katherine was no longer just looking into his eyes. The clarity between them had seeped into her mind and she was thinking, *Who was Dave Wenzel? I never heard the doorbell the first time. It never rang. Don Junior didn't see him go,*

Miss Korshak didn't see him come, Carleton Hare never saw him. I never saw his shadow, I never heard his voice. Don broke the window with the chair, and—the knife is unstained.

There never was a Dave Wenzel. My husband was hounded by an imaginary man—and now he has exorcised him by an imaginary murder.

"Dave Wenzel is dead," Don repeated. "He had to die—there was no other way. Do you want to call the police?"

She slowly shook her head.

"Good," he said. "That leaves just one more thing, Katherine. You must never ask me about him: who he was or how he died. We must never talk about him again."

Again she slowly nodded.

"And now," he said, "I'd like to go to bed. I'm really quite tired." He started toward the bedroom.

"Wait, Don," she said uncertainly. "The children—"

He turned in the bedroom door. "—are at Aunt Martha's," he finished for her, smiling sleepily. "Did you think I'd forgotten that, Kat?"

She shook her head and came toward him smiling, glad in the present, choking down the first of the thousand questions she would never be able to ask him.

Shadows

Pamela Sargent

The theme of alien invasions of Earth goes back to H. G. Wells and beyond; and here Pamela Sargent offers a novelette of Earth under the yoke of strange beings from the stars. But the purposes of conquest are many, and alien beings may conquer us for other than selfish reasons. How might we find that out, though?

Pamela Sargent is one of the strongest talents to enter science fiction in recent years. She has recently published her first novel, Cloned Lives.

The sun hid its face behind the clouds, a gray layered curtain which hung close to the Earth. Defeated, the city's inhabitants trudged along the highway, crowding the four lanes.

Suzanne Molitieri could hear the droning of murmurs punctuated by an occasional wail. *Don't look back.* She kept her eyes resolutely focused on the asphalt at her feet as she walked. Her hand clutched Joel's, both palms dry. Around her, people twisted their necks as they glanced back at the empty city.

Above them silver insects hovered, humming softly and casting faint shadows over the people below. They were passing the suburbs now and more people joined the stream, trickling down the highway entrances, creating small eddies before becoming part of the river. *Herded like animals.* Suzanne glanced at Joel, saw his brown eyes focused on her, and grasped his hand more tightly.

Resistance had been futile. A few invaders had been slaughtered by gunfire in Buenos Aires as they left their ship, and Buenos Aires had vanished, people and all. When the same thing happened in Canton and Washington, the will to resist had subsided. Suzanne doubted that it had completely vanished.

The Earth was an anthill to the Aadae. They had descended on it from the skies, stepping on it here and there when it was necessary. Yet Suzanne had seen an Aada in the city streets weeping over the dead burned bodies of some who had resisted. Then she and the others had been herded from the city, allowed to take nothing with them but the clothes they wore and a few personal possessions. Suzanne carried more clothes in a knapsack. She had left everything else behind; the past would be of no use to her now. Joel carried a pound of marijuana and some bottles of liquor in his knapsack; he was already planning for the future.

Suzanne adjusted the burden on her back. Around her the murmuring died and she heard only the sound of feet marching, treading the pavement with soft thuds. The conquered people moved past the rows of suburban houses which were silent witnesses to the procession.

Suzanne thought of empty turtle shells. The gun-metal gray domes surrounded her, covering the countryside in uneven rows. Groups of people huddled in front of each dome, waiting passively. She thought of burial mounds.

"How they get them up so fast?" A stocky black man standing near her was looking at a dome. He began to rub his hand across its gray surface. Suzanne could hear the sound of weeping. A plump pale woman next to Joel was whimpering, clinging to a barrel-chested man who was probably her husband.

"They took her kids away," a voice said. Suzanne found herself facing a slender black woman with hazel eyes. The woman's hair was coiled tightly around her head in cornrow braids. "She had six of them," the black woman went on. "They took them all to some other domes."

Suzanne, not knowing what to say, looked down at her feet, then back at the woman. "Did you have kids too?" she asked lamely.

"No, I always wanted to, but I'm glad now I didn't." The woman smiled bitterly and Suzanne felt that the subject was being dismissed. The stocky black man had wandered to the dome's triangular entrance. "I'm Felice Harrison," the woman muttered. "That's my husband Oscar." She waved at the man in the entrance.

"I'm Suzanne Molitieri." The introduction hung in the air between them. Suzanne wanted to giggle suddenly. Felice raised her eyebrows slightly.

"Are you all right?"

"I'm fine," said Suzanne, almost squeaking the words. Oscar joined his wife and placed his arm gently over her shoulders.

"This is Suzanne Molitieri," Felice said to Oscar, and Suzanne felt reassured by the steady smile on the man's broad face.

"I'm Joel Feldstein," Joel said quickly, and she felt his hand close around her waist. She had almost forgotten he was there. His hand seemed as heavy as a chain, binding her to him.

Joel smiled. His too-perfect teeth seemed to glitter; his brown eyes danced. With his free hand, he brushed back a lock of thick brown hair. *He's too beautiful,—I had to love him.* "I guess we're going to live in these things," Joel continued. "I can't figure it out, I don't understand these people. That's quite an admission for me; I've studied psychology for years. In fact, I was finishing my doctoral studies." *You haven't been near a classroom in years.* "I wanted to go into research, then marry Suzanne, give her a chance to finish school; she's been working much too hard helping me out." He smiled down at her regretfully. *Somebody had to pay the bills.* "The thing I regret most is not getting the chance to help Suzie." She winced at the nickname. The chainlike pressure on her waist tightened. "What about you two, what did you do?"

"It hardly matters now," Felice said dryly. Her hazel eyes and Oscar's black ones were expressionless.

"I guess you're right," said Joel. "You know, I even had a couple of papers published last year—I was really proud of that—but I guess that doesn't matter now either." *Why are you lying now?*

"I was a bus driver," said Oscar coldly. Suzanne suddenly felt that she was looking at the Harrisons across an abyss. Her mind began to clutch at words in desperation.

"What's it like inside the dome?" she said to Oscar. The black man seemed to relax slightly.

"Just a big room, with low tables and no chairs," Oscar answered. "Then there's these metal stairways winding around, and some rooms without doors, and the ceiling's glowing, don't ask me how. No lights, just this glow."

"Hey," Felice muttered. The people around them had

formed a line. Suzanne turned. One of the Aadae stood in front of them, holding a small metal device.

Suzanne sniffed at the air. She hadn't realized how smelly the Aadae actually were. She watched the alien and wondered again how the military must have felt when they first saw the conquerors.

The Aada appeared human, a small female not more than five feet tall and slender, with large violet eyes and pale golden skin. Her blue-black hair, uncombed and apparently unwashed, hung to her waist. She wore a dirty pair of bikini bottoms, spotted with stains. The alien scratched her stomach, and Suzanne almost snickered.

"Give nameh, go inside," said the Aada. She waved the metal rod she held at the dome. Then she pointed it at Joel. "Give nameh, go inside." The Aada's violet eyes stared past them, as if perceiving something else besides the line of people.

"Joel Feldstein." The rod was pointed at Suzanne.

"Suzanne Molitieri."

"Oscar Harrison."

"Felice Harrison." They began to move toward the dome.

"Are my children all right, please tell me, are they all right?" The plump mother of six was pleading with the alien.

"Nameh," the Aada repeated. Suzanne looked into the alien's violet eyes and was startled to see sadness there. The Aada's small golden hand patted the plump woman reassuringly. "Nameh," and the word this time seemed tinged by grief.

Puzzled, Suzanne turned away and entered the dome.

"You tell me," said Joel, "how a technologically advanced culture can produce such sloppy, dirty people. I can't get within two feet of one." He grimaced.

"Cleanliness and technological advancement aren't necessarily related," said Gabe Cardozo, shifting his plump body around on the floor. "Besides, from their point of view, they might be very neat. It depends on your perspective."

Suzanne, huddled against the wall near the doorless entrance to their room, suddenly felt dizzy. They had been drinking from one of Joel's bottles since early that evening. She tried to focus on the wall opposite the entrance.

The room was bare of furnishings except for two mats on the floor. A small closet near the door held their possessions. There was little space to move around in and she knew they were lucky to have the room to themselves. Gabe, two domes down, was sharing his room with three other people. She had asked Joel if they could have Gabe move in with them; he was, after all, Joel's best friend. But Joel had dismissed the idea, saying he had little enough privacy as it was. *No, you have to hide, Joel, that's it, Gabe might find out what you really are.*

"What do they want, anyway?" said Joel. "They took the trouble to put up these domes, I don't know how, moved us in, and we've been sitting around for three days with nothing to do." Joel suddenly laughed. "Whoever thought an alien invasion would be so goddamn boring."

"Well, they obviously don't need slave labor," Gabe said. "They put up these domes with no help and they are technologically advanced. And if they'd wanted the planet for themselves, I suppose they could have executed us. They want us for something, and they probably moved us out here so they could watch us more carefully. People could hide in the city."

"What difference does it make?" Suzanne said loudly, irritated by Gabe's professorial manner. "We'll find out sooner or later; what good does it do talking about it?" She stood up, wobbling a bit on weak-kneed legs. Gabe's walruslike moustache seemed to droop slightly; Joel shrugged his shoulders.

She found herself outside the room on the metal stairway, leaning forward, clutching the rail. The large room below her was empty and someone had pushed the low tables closer to the walls. She began to move down the stairs, still holding the rail. When she reached the bottom, she sat down abruptly on the floor, clutching her knees. "God," she whispered. The floor shifted under her.

A hand was on her shoulder. Startled, she looked up into Felice's hazel eyes. "Are you all right?"

"I'm fine," said Suzanne. "I don't know. I think I'm going to vomit."

"You need some air, come on." Suzanne stumbled to her feet. Holding on to Felice, she managed to get to the triangular doorway and outside.

A cool breeze bathed her face. "You better now?" asked Felice.

"I think so." She looked at the rows of lighted doorways in front of her. "You're up pretty late, Felice."

"I'm up pretty early. It's almost morning." Suzanne sighed and leaned against the dome. "You feel like taking a walk, honey?"

"Can we?" asked Suzanne. "Will they let us?"

"They haven't stopped me yet. No wonder you look so bad, staying inside for three days. Come on, we can walk to the highway; do you good."

"All right." Her head felt clearer already. She began to walk past the rows of domes with Felice. Occasionally, shadows moved across the triangular doorways they passed, transforming themselves into loose-limbed dancing scarecrows on the path in front of Suzanne.

"What's going to happen to us?" Suzanne muttered, expecting no answer. An apathetic calm had embraced her; her feet seemed to drag her behind them.

"Who knows, Suzanne? We wait, we find out about these

Aadae chicks, what their weak points are. That's all we can do. If we tried anything now, we got no chance. But we might later."

They reached the highway and stopped. Felice gestured at the domes across the road. "They live in those things too," she said to Suzanne. "I found out yesterday. I looked inside one of their doorways. Exactly like ours."

Suzanne looked toward the city. She could barely see the tall rectangles and spires of its skyline. To the left of the city, the early morning sky was beginning to glow. Felice clutched her arm and she noticed the Aadae for the first time. They were sitting on the highway in a semicircle, soundlessly gazing east.

"Suzanne." She swung around and saw Gabe, his face almost white. His dark frizzy hair was a cloud around his head. "Are you all right? I followed you just to be sure; you didn't look too well."

"I'm fine. Where's Joel?"

"He fell asleep. Or passed out. I'm not sure which." Gabe looked apologetic.

She shrugged, then looked uncertainly at Felice. "Oh, Gabe, this is—"

"I know Felice, she was in my evening lit class." Gabe smiled. "She was the best student in it."

Felice was appearing uncharacteristically shy. She grinned and looked down at her feet. "Come on," she said. "You were a good teacher, that's all." Suzanne shuddered at the mention of the past. *She watched Joel as he slept beside her. His slim, muscled chest rose and fell with each breath. I love you anyway, Joel; there's been more good than bad. We just need time, that's all; you'll find yourself.*

Suddenly she hated the Aadae. She closed her fists, hoping for an Aada's neck around which to squeeze them. Tears stung her eyes, blurring the image of the Aadae in the road.

"What are they doing?" Gabe whispered. She ignored him and began to walk along the highway toward the aliens. A soft sigh rose from the semicircle of Aadae and drifted to her. They were swaying now, back and forth from the waist.

The sun's edge appeared on the horizon, lighting up the road. The Aadae leaned forward. Suzanne, hearing footsteps behind her, stepped forward and turned.

Five pairs of blind violet eyes stared through her. Startled, she moved away from the five Aadae and let them pass. The five, dressed in dirty robes, stumbled onto the road, arms stretched in front of them. They wandered to the edge of the semicircle and stood there, holding their arms out toward the sun. Suzanne followed them and stood with them. They didn't seem to realize she was there.

She waved an arm in front of the nearest Aada. The alien showed no reaction. *They're truly blind*, she thought as she gazed into the empty eyes. The five Aadae continued to stare directly into the rising sun. They began to sway on their feet, burned-out retinas unable to focus. She stepped back from them, moving again to the side of the road.

Gabe and Felice were with her, pulling at her arms. "Come on," said Gabe, "we'd better get out of here, come on." She pulled her arms free and continued to watch the Aadae.

Something was drawing her toward the aliens, something that hovered over her, tugging at her mind. She was at peace, wanting only to join the group on the road. She found her head turning to the sun.

A shadow rose in front of her. "Suzanne!" It was Gabe, holding her by the shoulders. Suddenly she was frightened. She stumbled backward, grabbing at Gabe's arms. The sighs of the Aadae were louder now, driving her away.

"Run!" Suzanne screamed. "Run!" Her feet, pounding

along the side of the road, were carrying her back to the domes. She ran, soon losing herself among the domes. At last she stopped, exhausted, in front of one. She turned to the triangular doorway.

Two Aadae were there, one with stiff orange hair like a flame and shiny copper-colored skin. The dark-haired golden-skinned one was coming toward her. She threw up her arms, trying to ward her off.

The alien took her by the arm and tugged gently. Suzanne followed the Aada passively, led like a child along the path between the domes. Then they stopped and she realized that she was in front of her own dome.

She sighed and leaned against the doorway. Her fear had disappeared, and she was feeling a bit foolish. *I must have been really drunk.* The Aada released her, then bowed from the waist in an Oriental farewell before disappearing among the domes.

The air was heavy and the sky overcast. People were sitting or standing around aimlessly; occasionally small groups of people, scarcely speaking to each other, would pass by. Suzanne sat with her back to her dome, watching Felice mend a shirt. That morning, at breakfast, one of the men had stood up and thrown his bowl, still filled with greenish mush, at the wall. All of them had been growing tired of the food, which was always the same. But until today, they had simply gone to the slots on the wall, pushed the buttons, and passively accepted the green mush and milky blue liquid which were all the slots ever yielded besides glasses of water.

The green mush had stuck to the wall, resembling a fungoid growth. Rivulets ran from it, trickling to the floor. Then a tiny gray-haired woman hurled her bowl. Within seconds, everyone in the large room was throwing bowls and following the bowls with the glasses of blue liquid, shrieking with laughter as the liquid mingled with the mush on the walls. Several people hurried to the food slots and punched buttons wildly, pulled out more food and threw it at the walls. The orgy of food throwing had lasted almost half an hour until the walls were thickly coated and the Aadae had arrived.

The two aliens had ignored the mess. They brought a cart with them filled with oddly shaped metal objects of different sizes. One of the Aadae rummaged among the objects and removed a small cylinder. Then she held it over her head, showing it to everyone in the room. Her companion handed her a silvery block and the Aada attached it to the cylinder, then fastened a blue block to the cylinder's other end.

"Put together," the alien said, pointing with the object to the cart. The two Aadae turned and left the dome.

"What the hell," Suzanne heard Oscar mutter.

"We better do it," said the tiny old woman. "Who knows what they'll do if we don't."

The room was beginning to stink. A few flies buzzed near the mush-covered walls. "I'd better get Joel his breakfast," Suzanne said absently to Felice. She wandered over to the food slots, punched the buttons and removed a bowl and glass. People had already begun work on the objects by the time she was climbing the stairs to her room, where Joel still lay sleeping. *At least it's something to do.*

It had taken only a couple of hours to put the objects together. Once again, they were left with time on their hands, long hours that were chains on their minds, minutes through which they swam, pushed underwater, unable to come up for air. Felice was mending the shirt on her lap slowly and carefully; the sewing of each stitch became an entire project.

"They'll come back," said Suzanne. "And give us more pointless stuff to do."

"You know what I think," said the small black woman. "I think they're crazy. They don't need us to put that stuff together." Felice hunched herself over the shirt and continued sewing. "You can't even tell what the things are *for*."

Suzanne began to poke at a loose thread on her jeans. The humid air was making her sweat and her crotch was starting to itch. She had managed to wash her underwear by using several glasses of water from the food slots, but there was nowhere she could bathe except by one of the sinks in the bathroom where the water was always cold and anyone could wander in at any time. Suzanne was afraid to go to the bathroom alone anyway. A woman in one of the nearby domes had been raped in a bathroom; although her husband had beaten the man who had done it, the fear of rape had spread among many women. Now Suzanne went to the bathroom only with Joel or Felice or some of the other women in the dome. A couple of times Gabe would accompany her, looking modestly away from her at the wall while she squatted on the floor over the hole which would suck her wastes away down a large tube. There were no partitions between the holes; squatting over them had become ritualized, with everyone courteously avoiding a look at the others present in the bathroom. Occasionally there was moisture around the holes; someone had taken a piss and missed. One fastidious young couple tried to keep the bathroom clean, mopping the floor and walls with an old undershirt, but they were not always successful.

Suzanne was growing uneasy. She was used to seeing an occasional pair of Aadae stroll along the pathway in front of her, but the aliens seemed to have disappeared. Suddenly her muscles tightened involuntarily. Something was in the air, hovering over her, ready to pounce.

She heard a scream, a high-pitched, ululating sound, and then a roar, a bellowing from hundreds of throats. "Felice!"

she cried, grabbing at the woman next to her. Felice dropped her shirt and they both stood up.

We should go inside. Suzanne looked down the pathway and saw a large group of men moving toward the highway. She began to run toward them with Felice close behind her. Again she heard the scream, which had taken on the cadences of a mournful song. It was closer to her now. A small group of people had gathered in front of a dome up ahead. She ran to them and pushed her way through the crowd. Then she shrank back, moaning softly, slapping a hand over her mouth.

An Aada hung in the doorway by her feet. Someone had tied a rope around her ankles. The alien had been stabbed several times; brown clots covered her body. Her long orange hair brushed the ground as she turned in the doorway, her violet eyes stared sightlessly at the crowd. They were all that was left of her face, smashed by fists. Bone fragments protruded from her jaw; her copper-colored skin was covered by greenish bruises. On the ground beneath her lay another Aada, dying from wounds which covered her body. The alien on the ground drew her black hair over her chest, lifted her head slightly, and opened her mouth, and Suzanne again heard the song-like scream. Then she turned from them and was silent.

The people around Suzanne said nothing. She heard only their breathing, the sound of a giant bellows near a flame. She turned away from the alien bodies and stumbled back to Felice.

"We have to get out of here, Suzanne," she heard Felice whisper. Another roar reached her ears. She could see the crowd of men crossing the highway. Some of them had their arms raised. Knives glittered in their fists. An elongated shadow fell across the mob on the highway and she became conscious of a faint humming sound. An alien air vehicle was in the sky, a slender silver torpedo waiting to pounce.

A bright light flashed across the highway soundlessly. She threw an arm across her eyes and staggered backward. The people in front of the dome were running past her. An arm swung out and hit her, knocking her onto the path. She climbed to her feet, looking aimlessly around. The air vehicle was moving away to the north.

"Felice!" she cried out. Her voice shook. Then she saw that there were no longer any men on the highway, only burned, blackened bodies strewn about on the asphalt. The smell of charred flesh was carried to her nostrils and she bent over, vomiting quietly, arms wrapped around her shaking body.

"The fools." It was Felice's voice, harsh and bitter. "Too soon." A hand was on her shoulder, pulling at her gently. She looked over at Felice, then back at the highway.

A group of Aadae were there, looking down at the bodies. *Happy, aren't you? It wasn't even a contest.* There was no way now to tell who lay in the road, if anyone she knew was there. She would have to wait, find out who was missing, and that would take days. Any mourning would be general and unfocused. The Aadae began to circle around the bodies.

Then she heard the sobbing, deep and uncontrolled weeping. Three Aadae threw themselves down on the pavement, beating against it with their fists. The aliens were crying, not for the two Aadae who had been murdered, but for the men on the highway.

Felice was pulling her back along the pathway toward their own dome. As they retreated, Suzanne caught one last glimpse of the Aadae as they flung their arms open to the sun and heard once again their musical scream.

She heard Joel as he crept toward his mat in the darkness. She turned over and reached for him, brushing against his leg. He jumped back. "Jesus! Don't scare me like that."

"Joel, where have you been?"

"Where I was the night before."

"Where?"

"None of your goddamn business, Suzanne." He pulled off his clothes and sprawled on the mat next to hers.

"I just want to know, Joel."

"I can tell you're back to normal; you're going to revive the Inquisition. I'm tired. I'm going to sleep."

"You haven't gotten up one morning this week, Joel, ever since they started giving us that stuff to put together."

"I should care. You don't even know what the fuckers are *for*, you just sit there putting them together, you think it's really important, don't you, just like that dumb job at the warehouse you used to have."

"It's not that, Joel. They're going to find out you're not doing your share, and God knows what they'll do then."

"I could give a shit." She could hear him turn over on his mat and knew the conversation was finished. Suzanne had heard rumors about a group of men and a few women who would meet late at night to discuss what to do about the Aadae. She knew nothing more and was afraid to know even that much. She remembered the burned bodies on the highway and decided it was best simply to go about her business and wait.

She was pretty sure that Oscar Harrison was in the group and that Felice knew about it, although she doubted that the protective Oscar would allow his wife to go to the meetings. It wouldn't be hard for her to get involved if she wanted, but she preferred to wait and see if anything happened. She could act then.

"*It's a perfectly good job, Joel; why are you always putting it down?*" She put down her beer and glared at him across the kitchen table.

"*It's a dead end and you know it. That's all life is for you, getting by. You could do more and you know it, but it's easier this way—you don't have to think or try. It's even easier to put up with me; it's better than being alone. At least I know what I am; you don't even look at yourself.*"

I was practical, at least. Not that it mattered now. There had been no more money for her training in music, so she had left school and taken the job in the warehouse office, telling herself it was only temporary, she could still have her voice lessons, go to the local opera company's rehearsals at night. But she stopped going to the rehearsals—she was usually too tired—and then she had stopped going to the voice lessons. *I wouldn't have been much good anyway.* Occasionally she sang for her friends at parties, smiling when they told her she should become a professional; *it's just a hobby.* Then Gabe had rushed over one day to tell her that the opera was holding auditions, they needed a new soprano, she would be perfect, the pay wasn't much, but she could at least quit that office job. And she promised to go to the audition, but by then she was out of training, her voice roughened by cigarettes, so she didn't go after all. There was no point to it. She had just gotten a raise; no sense in throwing it away.

It doesn't matter. The Aadae were here and had no use for singers, nor for office workers. Her past was a meaningless memory, her possible future in that other world only a shadow of the wishes that had once crossed her mind. Better that she had had no great ambitions when the Aadae came; she would not have been able to stand it. Her dreams had already died. *It's just as well.*

The orange-haired alien was named Neir-let. Felice had mentioned that to her a couple of days before. Neir-let and her dark-haired companion were the Aadae who had instructed them in how to put together the metal objects which were now beginning to clutter the large downstairs room of the dome. Neir-let wore a blue gem on her forehead, seemingly embedded in her skin, as did all the other Aadae. Suzanne hadn't even noticed this until Oscar had pointed it out; most of the aliens' foreheads were covered by their untidy hair. The gem was tiny, smaller than a Hindu's caste mark; it glittered, and Suzanne shivered involuntarily.

Neir-let had become more fluent in English, although no one could be sure about how she had learned it. Her companion never said anything. Neir-let had just demonstrated how to attach a silver globe to the apparatus they had been building, then she gave them a cartful of silver globes, several of which went rolling out of the cart over the floor, stopping their travels under the food slots. The metal objects on the floor were entwined in metallic tubing; the blocks and cylinders they had started out with were already hidden. The silver globes were to be attached to some of the loose ends of tubing.

Suzanne, sitting with Felice and a red-headed woman named Asenath Berry at one of the tables, reached for her bowl of mush. She was losing weight. Suzanne had already been thin before the Aadae came. On the diet of mush, she estimated, from the looseness of her clothing, that she had lost another ten pounds. A *scarecrow*. Her brown hair, always unruly, stood out around her head like a nimbus; there was no way to straighten it here.

No one made any move toward the objects they were supposed to be putting together. They had all learned that Neir-let was fairly easy going and didn't seem to care what they did as long as the work was completed by the evening. Neir-let was sitting on the floor near the doorway, picking what looked like small insects out of her hair. Her companion leaned against the wall, scratching her crotch.

Suddenly Oscar stood up and walked over to Neir-let. Suzanne glanced at Felice. The chatter in the large room died down. No one had dared to approach an alien directly up to now. Asenath Berry poked Suzanne in the ribs. "What the hell is he up to?" the redhead asked. Suzanne shrugged. Asenath had lost little weight on the mush diet; her round, braless breasts were an edifice under her sleeveless blue top and Suzanne wondered if Asenath had used silicone. Her long tanned legs were set off by her white shorts. How she kept them shaved was a mystery. Felice had said that Asenath was a prostitute, that she had come out of the city with a closetful of clothes and cosmetics carried by three of her most faithful customers. Asenath shared her room with a lean black man named Warren, who, like Joel, usually slept late. "A mack," Felice had told her, sneering at the word. *What do I care.* Suzanne had met Asenath one night in the hallway. The redhead had taken one look at her frail figure and pulled out two cans of beef stew hidden in her purse. "You need them more than me, honey." She had hurried back to her room to share them with Joel, who opened them with his knife, and they had eaten them slowly, relishing each bite. Since then, she found it difficult not to be friendly to Asenath, although at the same time she was a bit frightened of her.

"I just want to ask a question," Oscar said to Neir-let. The room was silent. Neir-let looked up at Oscar and smiled. "I just want to know what that blue thing in your head is."

The alien was still smiling. "Through it I am with those above," she replied, and shrugged as if that were self-explanatory.

"The others of your kind?" Oscar said slowly.

"No, except . . ." Neir-let paused. "I have no words." She smiled at Oscar and raised her hands, palms up. Oscar nodded and returned to Felice's side, looking thoughtful.

A few people got up and began to attach the globes to some of the metal objects strewn across the floor. "I think they still have spaceships overhead," said Oscar to Felice, "and she means they can contact them with those blue stones. That's all it could mean. At any sign of trouble, they could wipe us all out." He clenched his fists. Asenath was smiling at a burly man seated at the next table. Suzanne ate her mush, licking it off her fingers, forcing herself. Asenath stood up, motioned to the burly man, and left the room with him. The Aadae were paying no attention.

Somebody should do something. She finished the mush and looked around. Everyone was devoting full attention either to the breakfast mush or to the metal objects. Neir-let and her friend had moved outside and were staring up at the sky. Suzanne's arms seemed to freeze on the table near her empty bowl. She was unable to move, eyes fixed on her fingertips. Thoughts were chasing each other through her mind; she could grasp none of them. A heavy weight was pushing her against the table, preventing her from standing up and going to work on the metal devices.

Someone nudged her. "That ho's lookin' for you," Felice drawled contemptuously. She forced herself to look up and saw Asenath on the metal stairway, motioning to her. The burly man had disappeared. "Don't go," Felice went on. "You don't want to be with the likes of her." Then Oscar put a restraining hand on his wife's shoulder.

"Don't tell Suzanne what to do," he said quietly. "You go ahead," he said to Suzanne. She hesitated for a moment, then got up and walked to the stairway.

"Come on up," she called to Suzanne. She climbed the stairs.

"What is it?"

"I got two packs of cigarettes off my friend," Asenath

whispered. She winked at Suzanne and her black eyelashes seemed to crawl over her eye like an insect. "Want a couple?"

"That was fast work," Suzanne said, trying to smile. Asenath's cold blue eyes showed no reaction.

"You better come to my room, or else everybody's going to want one." The redhead turned and Suzanne followed her past the first level of rooms and up the next flight of stairs. Asenath finally stopped in front of a doorway. "Come on in." Suzanne entered the room. Warren was sprawled across his mat, clothed in a pink shirt and velvety purple slacks. He held a small hand mirror and was fiddling with his moustache. "Have a seat," said Asenath, motioning to her mat. Suzanne sat, feeling uneasy.

Asenath didn't sit down. She peered out into the hallway, then strode over to Suzanne. "There aren't any cigarettes, kid, just some questions."

Suzanne opened her mouth. Her vocal chords locked and nothing emerged except a sharp gasp. She swallowed and pulled her legs closer to her chest.

"What's that man of yours been up to?" asked Asenath.

"I don't know," she managed to say. "I don't know what you mean." Her voice sounded weak, ineffectual.

"Stop being stupid. He's been out every night this week, we know that, and we know where he is for some of the time. Now you tell us where he goes."

"I don't know."

"You're saying that a little too often; I don't want to hear it again. We've tried following him. We know he doesn't come back here right away. You must know something, he must have hinted at what he does."

Suzanne looked away from Asenath to Warren, who had put down his hand mirror and was staring blankly at the wall. "I don't know where he goes," she said, pronouncing the words carefully. "I don't know anything about his activities. Joel tells me nothing. He rarely told me anything, even before we all came here. Our relationship is not exactly what you would call open." She felt defeated and exposed before the red-headed woman and her dark silent partner.

"Christ," Asenath muttered.

"Let her go," said Warren. Suzanne stood up and began to move toward the door. A hand seized her shoulder and she found herself facing Asenath's blue eyes again.

"If you do find out anything," the prostitute whispered, "if he does decide to confide in you, you better let me know, I'm telling you, and right away. And you just keep quiet about this little talk."

She retreated from the room angry and frightened, afraid to stop now in her own room to wake up Joel. *I have to warn him. I have to find out. I have to talk to somebody.* She paused at the top of the stairway, apprehensive about joining the people in the large room below. But they were ignoring her, busy working on their alien devices.

She continued down the steps, avoiding a glance at Felice and Oscar. She sat down in a corner and began fitting metal pieces together under the casual, almost reassuring gaze of Neir-let.

"I have to talk to you, Gabe."

"Sure."

"Not here." Suzanne eyed the people sitting in front of Gabe's dome nervously and felt that they were all watching her. She forced herself to look at them directly and realized that they were paying her little attention. "I mean, I feel like walking around."

"Okay." Gabe hoisted himself off the ground and brushed off his dirty rumpled trousers. Oddly enough, he seemed to be maintaining his girth on the Aadaen diet. He took her arm gently. "Back to your room?"

"Joel's there. I mean, I think he's still asleep." She recognized a face in front of one of the domes and waved at it while nodding her head. "Let's walk on the highway."

The weather was warm but not humid. White clouds danced across the blue sky under the benevolent gaze of the sun. A group of adolescent boys had somehow gotten hold of a baseball and bat and were playing a game on the highway. Farther down the road, Suzanne could see a group of children with some Aadae. They too were playing a game, chasing what looked like cylinders on wheels across the safety islands. Suzanne and Gabe walked toward the city, past the baseball players.

"I have to talk about Joel," she said. "I'm worried."

"What's the problem this time?"

"It isn't just a personal thing, Gabe. I'm scared. Joel's been out nights, I don't know where he goes. Maybe it's none of my business, I guess I should be used to it by now. But the thing is . . ." She lowered her voice. "A couple of other people want to know where he goes too, Gabe; they were asking me about it this morning. They weren't being gentle. I think they would have beaten it out of me if they thought I knew."

Gabe scratched at his beard. In the absence of razor blades he, like most of the men, was looking shaggier than usual. "You don't know where he goes?"

"For God's sake, Gabe. No, I don't. I thought you might. I thought you could tell me what's going on."

"I think you should tell me who wanted to know about Joel, Suzanne."

"Asenath Berry. You've seen her, the good-looking redhead, the whore. She and her friend Warren wanted to know. I was dumb enough to think Asenath wanted to be my friend."

Gabe sighed and was silent for a few seconds. She could hear the shouts of the baseball-playing boys in back of them. "I'll talk to her," Gabe said at last. "She won't bother you again."

"Then you do know something." She stopped walking and faced him. "Tell me. What is it?"

"I shouldn't tell you. I tried not to; I thought it was best that you stay out of it. But I guess you have a right to know. A group of us have been making some plans; that's all I can say. Joel's part of the group. So is Asenath. Some of us have been a little suspicious of Joel lately. It seems he doesn't go directly home from our little get-togethers. Asenath must have taken it upon herself to find out."

She turned away from Gabe, bewildered. "Now I've just upset you," he muttered. "It's probably nothing. We're all a little paranoid; we have to be. We'll probably find out he's just visiting a friend or something. Don't worry, he's not that involved with us anyway; we've been holding meetings without him once in a while. I don't think he wants to get tangled up in anything too dangerous. You know Joel."

Gabe was leaving something out. Suddenly she didn't want to hear any more, didn't want to know what Gabe or Joel or anyone else might be planning. "He's seeing someone else," she said. "He's seeing another girl. It's happened before." *That must be it.* The thought left her empty, almost relieved.

"Why do you stay with him, Suzanne?"

"I don't know. What difference does it make now?" She turned to the city. "Let's just keep walking, Gabe, let's go back to the city; they'll never find us there, we'll get Joel and go back and we can sit around drinking at Mojo's like we used to."

"You know we can't."

"Why not?"

"They'll find us. We should go back, Suzanne. Come on, I'll walk you to your dome."

"I'd rather not go back there right now," she said wearily. She went to the side of the road and sat down on some grass. "You can leave if you want, Gabe, I think I'd rather be alone right now anyway."

"You're sure, Suzanne? You'll be okay?"

"I'll be fine."

"You won't do anything silly?"

"No."

"Well, if you want to talk to me later or anything, feel free." She watched him shuffle back down the highway, shoulders slumped forward.

She pulled at the grass near her foot. Things were slipping away from her again as they always had. Her relationship with Joel had always seemed fortuitous. He had drifted into her life at a party she almost didn't attend; he could very well drift out again and there was nothing she could do about it. At worst he would get involved in some foolhardy scheme with Gabe and the others, resulting in disaster; she was convinced that the Aadae could not be defeated. At best, he would stay with her and they would continue living in the dome as they had with no purpose other than constructing alien objects for the Aadae. The thought made her shudder. It was useless to look ahead; the best thing to do was to get through each day, forfeiting any hopes. She had practice at that already.

A cloud danced in front of the sun, shadowing the road in front of her. She shivered in the cooler air.

Joel had disappeared again. In the morning, his mat was empty. Suzanne, awake at dawn, was outside the dome, shivering slightly in the wet air.

A heavy fog hung over the domed settlement, its gray masses almost indistinguishable from the metal domes. Its tendrils wound along the pathway and wrapped themselves around her feet. Suzanne stepped away from the doorway into the fog and was soon lost in its billowing masses, unable to see more than dim shapes. She was hidden and protected.

She was not looking for Joel. She didn't really want to know where he was and didn't want to risk confronting him in the presence of someone else. She tried to think about him objectively in the gray silence. It was foolish to think she could be everything to him, that she could fulfill all his needs, particularly in the present situation. He had always come back before. She demanded little sexually, content to satisfy Joel's needs with few of her own. She thought of Paul, whom she had loved while still in school. After two months, she had finally allowed Paul to share her cot in the dormitory room, twisting against him frantically during the night. She had satisfied him, but not herself. She avoided Paul after that. There was another, a boy whose name she couldn't remember, at a party, and with him there were only spasms and a drained, nauseous feeling afterward. With Joel she acted, going through the motions but always distant, her mind drifting off as he entered her. At times she would feel a twinge or an occasional spasm. She knew she loved him, or at least had loved him once; yet if he had remained with her, never touching her except for a kiss or a few hugs, she would have been content. *I can't expect him to be satisfied with that; no one would be. Why shouldn't he see someone else? It's surprising he stays with me at all.* Her heart twisted at the thought. Her mind throbbed, recoiling from the image of Joel with a vague female shape, and tears stung her eyes. She hated her body, a piece of perambulating dead meat, an anesthetized machine. *No, not anesthetized.* She could, after all, feel pain.

She was lost in the fog. She no longer knew where her own dome was. She kept walking, thinking that if she could find the highway, she could reorient herself.

"Hey." She turned. "Hey." Two young black men stood in the doorway of a dome, watching her. They were smiling, and one of them gestured to her. She fled into the fog, turning down another path and almost running until she was sure the two men were far behind. Then she suddenly felt shame. *They probably just wanted to ask me something.* She shook off the thought. *I have to be careful.* But she wondered if she would have hurried away if the men had been white. Her cheeks burned.

She was more lost than before. She stopped in front of a dome and tried to figure out where she was. She should have come to the highway by now.

She peered inside the dome tentatively, then stepped back. It was guarded by two Aadae. Inside, she could see aliens sleeping on the floor in the large central room. She had not seen the inside of one of their dwellings before, afraid of approaching one. The guards looked at her inquisitively. She backed away farther, trying to smile harmlessly, then continued on the path.

She collided with someone. She opened her mouth to apologize, then threw her hands in front of her face and managed to suppress a scream. A bald, wizened figure stood there, clad only in a dirty robe. It was no more than five feet tall and its greenish-yellow skin was stretched tightly over bones. It stared at her blankly and she recognized the violet eyes of the Aadae. Its robe hung open, revealing a penis no thicker than a finger. The blue stone on its forehead seemed to wink at her.

One of the males. She felt nauseous. The figure tried to reach for her, his lips drawing back across his teeth in an imitation of a smile. She moved back, trying to ward him off with her arms.

Then another Aada was beside him, holding his arm. She recognized Neir-let. The Aada was whispering to the male in her own language. The male, still grinning, sat down.

"He frightens you?" Neir-let asked. Suzanne sighed with relief. "He is harmless."

"I didn't know . . . I haven't seen a male Aada before."

Neir-let looked puzzled for a second, then nodded. "Male. We have few, enough for children. We always have few. This one is old and no longer wise." The male was drooling and picking at his toenails. "Soon his mind will join the others above. In his travels, he may see our home again." Neir-let sat down with the male, her arm across his shoulders.

"Do you miss your home?" Suzanne said impulsively. She was suddenly curious about the Aadae, who as far as she knew rarely talked to anyone. Neir-let seemed to sigh.

"To you, Suzanne, I will talk," said the alien. She was shocked, not realizing that Neir-let knew her name. "You have a gift, I know. You have brushed those above once in the dawn. Do you remember? You fled from us."

Suzanne struggled with her memories, then recalled the morning she had seen the Aadae seated on the highway, staring into the sun. She nodded silently.

"Yes, I miss my home. I will not see it again as I am. But I could not stay there knowing that other minds would die. Your world is much like ours, but the small differences bring me sadness. Yet I could live here with my daughters and be pleased." Neir-let paused. Suzanne sat down near her, for once unafraid. "But we must leave here and the home of my daughters must be the ship."

Leave here. If we wait long enough . . . "Why are you here?" she asked.

"So that you will not die."

"You've killed so many of us, though. Why?"

Tears glistened in the alien's eyes. "If we had not, others would have joined them. Then all of you would die. It is a painful thing, Suzanne." Neir-let patted the male alien on the head and trilled to him. He nestled against her. Suzanne was at peace, strangely, not wanting to leave Neir-let's side. The fog had lifted slightly. *I should get back to the dome*, she thought, unwilling to move.

From the corner of her eye, she saw a shape leave the doorway of the dome where the Aadae slept. She turned to face it. *Joel.* The shape disappeared in the fog and she could not be sure.

Neir-let was still singing to the male Aada. Suzanne rose and began to thread her way through the maze of paths. She could see more clearly now and soon managed to find her own dome.

She hurried inside and up the stairway. In her room, Joel lay on his mat, seemingly asleep. Yet his breathing was shallow and his hair and face were dotted with small beads of moisture. She wanted to speak to him, to question him. She clamped her lips shut and curled up on her own mat, nursing her pain and her fear.

She had to talk to Gabe. She had to tell him what Neir-let had said.

She went looking for him as soon as she was through with her work for the day. The bright sunlight had burned away the fog of that morning and by noon the weather was hot and humid. A group of people, among them Oscar Harrison and Asenath Berry, had gathered in front of the dome when she left, speaking to each other in low, angry tones. One man reached out and grabbed her as she passed and she tried to pull away.

"Let her go," said Oscar. The man released her. Suzanne retreated, then looked back. Everyone in the area seemed to be leaving the vicinity as if expecting trouble. Joel was still asleep upstairs and for a moment she wondered if she should go back and wake him up. *Better to let him sleep; he'll miss the trouble.* She went on to Gabe's dome.

Gabe was not in his room. One of his roommates, a frail-looking Chinese man named Soong, looked up as she entered.

"Do you know where Gabe is?" she asked him. "I have to talk to him." She felt impatient, on edge. "It's pretty important."

Mr. Soong smiled. "He is being entertained by a young lady, I believe, a few domes down. He has been away all night. You can find him there, but I do not know if he wishes to be disturbed."

The old windbag. "Which dome?"

"I am not sure. If you wish to wait here, you are welcome. Please be seated." The man nodded toward one of the mats which crowded the floor. "Gabe was indeed overwhelmed by good fortune. He was surprised when the young lady appeared last night and invited him to share her company. Usually he is back by morning, but she was a very attractive woman."

And he's always complaining about his lousy luck. "Thank you," said Suzanne, trying to be as dignified as Mr. Soong. "I'll come back later. Please tell him Suzanne's looking for him; he'll know who I am."

She went back out the door and down the stairway. She paused in the downstairs room, wondering if she should talk to Felice. Then she remembered the angry crowd in front of her dome. *I can't go back there.*

For the first time, it occurred to her that Neir-let might have spoken to her in confidence. Perhaps she didn't want Suzanne speaking to anyone else about their talk; maybe she would be angry if she found out she had. She shrugged off the idea. It couldn't hurt to tell someone and it might prevent them from acting rashly. She remembered the burned bodies on the highway. They could afford to wait, knowing that the Aadae planned to leave.

"Suzanne." Gabe was standing in the doorway. She hurried toward him. He was smiling contentedly. "I finally had some luck, this girl I hardly know . . ."

"Mr. Soong told me." She tried to smile back.

"Don't look so irritated. I'll start flattering myself by thinking you're jealous."

"Gabe, I have to talk to you. I was talking to one of the Aadae last night and she told me they were going to leave eventually, I don't know when, but that's what she said."

"Where did you see her?"

"I just happened to run into her, I was wandering around. Gabe, if we can just wait . . ."

"Suzanne, they won't leave until they've accomplished their purpose, whatever that is. It could be pretty hideous, you know."

"Neir-let said they want to keep us from dying."

Gabe wiped his forehead with the back of his hand. "No doubt she was speaking figuratively."

Someone outside was shouting. Suzanne shook her head and began to move toward the doorway. "What's going on," she said listlessly. Something seemed to be keeping her from looking outside.

Gabe was pulling at her hand. "Don't talk to Neir-let any more," he muttered. "In fact, I wouldn't advise talking to any of the Aadae unless you can't help it. Some people don't like it; you could get into trouble."

She was suddenly annoyed by Gabe. She withdrew her hand and went outside. A small group of people were standing in front of her dome. She wandered toward them. Something was in the doorway of the dome. She moved closer.

She saw Joel. A shock seemed to strike her body, paralyzing her. Blood rushed to her head and face. Her skin crawled over her stiff muscles, a cold piece of iron was resting in her belly. Joel was hanging by his neck in the doorway. He had been stabbed several times. Someone had ripped off his shirt, revealing long scratches on his chest. His feet dangled loosely from his legs. Above him, someone had posted a sign: COL-LABORATOR. His eyes were closed, the long lashes shadowing his cheekbones.

She began to push people aside as she walked to the doorway. She stumbled near a knife carelessly abandoned under the slowly rotating body. She picked up the bloodstained weapon and began to hack at the rope that held Joel by the neck.

"Suzanne." Gabe was near her. His voice seemed to reach her ears from a distance. "Come away from here." She continued to cut the rope until the body fell at her feet, a flesh-covered sack of bones. One hand draped itself across her left ankle, then slipped away.

She stepped over the body into the large central room. No one was there. Unfinished metal devices were strewn across the floor. She heard footsteps clatter near her and turned around.

Asenath Berry crouched on the stairway. Her blue eyes were hidden behind dark glasses. The redhead had a large knapsack on her back. Suzanne moved toward her, still holding the knife.

"Wait!" shouted Asenath, holding up her arms. "He told us everything before he died—he admitted it—we made sure of that. He told them everything he knew about our group, about our plans. They promised him a reward." Asenath continued to creep down the stairs. "He was a traitor, do you understand? He was looking out for himself."

The redhead was only a few feet away from her. Suzanne lunged toward Asenath, knocking her on her side. She lifted the knife. Asenath's foot hit her hand, knocking the knife across the room. The redhead tried to climb to her feet. Suzanne grabbed the curly red hair and began to pull at it silently.

Hands clawed at Suzanne's legs. "Stop it!" Asenath was screaming. Holding the prostitute's head with one hand, she started to punch her in the breasts.

"For God's sake!" Gabe's big arms were around her, pulling her away from Asenath. She sagged against him, suddenly exhausted, staring at the clump of red hair in her left hand. Asenath got up and scrambled out the door.

Gabe was shaking her by the shoulders. She managed to get free and saw the knife against the wall near the stairway. She picked it up and tucked it under her belt. Then she walked outside.

The small crowd was still there. Ignoring them, she grabbed Joel's feet and began to drag him along the pathway behind her. The people moved away from her, receding until she could see no faces, only blurs. She dragged Joel past the gray domes until she reached the side of the highway. She collapsed next to him, one arm across his chest.

I should have been with you. She drew his head near her chest. *I should have helped you. I didn't even talk to you. I didn't even try to find out what was wrong.*

She waited, watching the body, thinking that he would start to breathe again, that he would speak and hold out his arms to her. *You once told me you were a survivor, you would live forever.* He would hold on to her and she would take him back to the dome and help him recover.

She waited. A few people hurried past her and on down

the highway, toward the city. They were leaving, ready to make plans and take their chances away from the domed settlement.

She waited. Joel did not move, did not speak. She began to dig his grave in the dirt, scratching at the soil with her knife and hands. She continued to dig until her hands were bleeding and her shoulders were stiff and sore.

She looked up. The sun had drifted to the west. Joel was covered by evening shadows. Overhead, the silvery aircraft of the Aadae hummed past, heading for the city. She stood up, staggering a little, and watched them.

The towers of the city gleamed. Several aircraft were hovering over them, insects over a crown. The sudden flash of light almost blinded her. She stumbled backward, closing her eyes.

When she opened them, she saw only blackened ruins where the city had been. Then the charred hulks collapsed before her eyes and she saw only a burned-out pit. Nearby, she could hear the strange mourning cry of the Aadae.

She dropped to her knees and began once more to dig.

Suzanne lay in her room. Now and then, she heard footsteps pass the door. Bits of conversation would drift from the main room up the stairs to her. She lay on her mat, her arms and legs held down by invisible bonds. Occasionally she slept.

Time became waves washing over her gently. She floated, occasionally focusing her eyes on the ceiling. A dark shape with flaming hair leaned over her and she saw it was Neir-let. "We must finish our task," the alien whispered. "Please help." She closed her eyes and when she opened them again, the Aada had disappeared.

Joel was near. She could tell that he was trying to be silent so he wouldn't disturb her. He was rummaging in the kitchen, trying to cook the blueberry waffles he had surprised her with one Sunday morning. She turned on her side and saw Gabe sitting against the wall.

"I didn't know what they were going to do," he said. "It was a trick, that girl taking me to her room; they knew I was his friend; they didn't want me around." She opened her mouth, trying to speak. Her lips were cracked and dry. *Don't worry*, she wanted to say, *you can stay for breakfast; Joel doesn't mind.* She closed her eyes and felt a wet cloth on her face.

When she woke up again, she was lying under a long coat. Someone had removed her clothes. "I washed you off," said Gabe. He was holding a glass of blue liquid. He lifted her head and helped her sip some of it.

"How long have I been here?" she managed to ask.

"Days. I thought you were going to die." He put her head back on the mat.

"No, I won't die." She looked at her arm on top of the coat. Her hands had become bony claws, the blue veins which covered her arm were a web. "I won't die," she said again, in despair.

"I'll stay with you if you want me," said Gabe. "I moved into the room next door, but if you want me here, I'll stay. Just tell me."

She shook her head, rolling it from side to side on the mat. "No."

"Think it over, at least." He patted her hand. She withdrew it from him slowly and placed it under the coat.

"No." She was floating now. The room grew darker and the walls seemed to shimmer. Again she felt a wet cloth on her face.

When she woke up once more, Gabe was gone.

• •

Suzanne wandered through the large downstairs room and took a seat next to the wall. She gazed at the people sitting around the tables. The tiny gray-haired woman was absent. Warren, Asenath, Oscar, and Felice were gone, as were others she had known only by sight: a big red-haired fellow, a bony middle-aged blonde, an acne-scarred Puerto Rican. She remembered the burned city, and then Joel.

She picked up one of the metal devices near her. Three cylinders, woven together with metallic tubing, were joined to three globes. The cylinders rested on golden rectangular bases. The whole apparatus was about three feet in height. She wondered absently if they would ever be finished. She put the device down and waited for the Aadae to arrive with more components.

She resumed watching the people at the tables. It was possible that some of them, even now, were planning a way to resist or defeat the aliens, but she doubted it. The city was still too vivid an example in their minds, most likely. Most of the resisters, the determined and forceful ones, had probably died there. *This crowd's like me*, she thought bitterly. *We'll get by.* She noticed that some of the people appeared uneasy and realized that she was glaring at them. She looked away.

Gabe's heavy denimed legs were in front of her. She waved him away, but he sat down in front of her anyway.

"You had any breakfast, Suzanne?"

"No."

"You should eat. If you want, I'll get you some."

"I ate last night; I don't want anything now." She didn't tell him she had vomited the meal in the bathroom, kneeling on the floor and holding her hair off her face with one hand. "Thanks anyway, Gabe," she said tonelessly. He seemed to expand visibly at that, as if taking her words as encouragement. He hovered over her like a beast of prey, his brown beard making her think of a grizzly bear. She hated him at that moment. *Always sniffing around; you wanted Joel to die, you son of a bitch.* She was quickly ashamed of herself. *He's just trying to help.* She grew conscious of the hairy legs concealed by her dungarees, and her halitosis; one of her teeth, with no dental care, was slowly, painfully, and aromatically rotting away. She almost chuckled at the thought of Gabe, or anyone else, desiring her sexually. She folded her arms across her breasts, *knobby little things,* and again thought of Joel and all the ways in which she had failed him. Yet part of her still knew that regret was her justification, enjoyable for those who were seasoned to it, a way of believing that things could have been different. *Give me a thousand chances, and I would be the same.* That thought too had its comforting aspects. Her mind curled up inside her and continued its self-flagellation with the willows of guilt, leaving its peculiarly painful and pleasurable scars.

Gabe jostled her elbow. Neir-let and her companion were at the doorway, but this time they brought no components, only two small leatherlike pouches. Neir-let surveyed the room, apparently waiting for everyone's full attention, then she began to speak in her musical voice.

"We have almost finished assembly of these tools," she said. Suzanne straightened her back at the words. "Only one thing remains." The alien leaned over and picked up one of the metal objects. "Each of you should select one now, and keep it with you at all times." Suzanne reached over for the one she had handled before and watched as everyone scrambled about. No one appeared angry or relieved; they clutched the objects passively and silently, then retreated to the walls, seating themselves on the floor.

Neir-let opened her pouch and took out a small blue gem. It winked in the light and was seemingly answered by the blue stone embedded in Neir-let's forehead. "You will place this in the small dent you will find in one of the globes. It will adhere to the surface by itself." Neir-let and the other Aada began to move around the room, handing a blue stone to each person. Suzanne accepted hers from Neir-let and soon found the dented globe. She pressed the stone into the dent and waited.

The task was completed by everyone in a few minutes. Neir-let walked back to the doorway and held up her arms. "What I tell you now will be the hardest thing to do," she said. "You must sit with these tools and wait, concentrating on them as much as you are able. You may go outside if you wish, or sit by the road. If you grow weary, rest, then. try again."

The two Aadae left the dome. Suzanne got up and began to follow them with her device. Gabe caught her by the arm.

"Where are you going?"

"Outside to concentrate," she replied. "What else can I do?"

"Don't. I wouldn't be surprised if they were trying to turn us into a group of zombies. Forget it. Let them try to force us; there's no way you can compel a person to concentrate."

She pulled away from him and went outside. She didn't care about the device. She wanted to get away from Gabe and the dome, sit alone with her thoughts. She walked toward the highway and seated herself next to the mound under which Joel lay. She would keep her vigil with him.

She put the metal object down at her side and found herself distracted by the blue gem. It seemed to tug at her mind, drawing her attention to itself. She continued to stare at the stone, secure in its blue gaze. Her mind was steady, hovering over her body, able to look at the grave near her with no sadness. She was at peace.

Somehow she managed to withdraw from the object. She rose unsteadily to her feet. It was almost noon. Her feet were asleep, her back stiff. She stomped around, trying to restore her circulation.

"Suzanne." Neir-let was standing by the mound. "You have seen?"

"What is this thing? What does it do, Neir-let?" It was the first time she had addressed the Aada by name and her tongue slid uncertainly over the words.

"It is a tool to build strength. It will aid you, but in a short time you will not need it, I think."

Suzanne turned from the alien, and noticed that a group of boys were playing baseball on the highway, while others sat on the side of the road in conversation. She saw only one woman, outside a dome, concentrating on her device. "No one else seems to be bothering."

"It does not matter," Neir-let said. "One, or a few, will lead and they must follow. You will see. A few are more receptive."

Suzanne sat down again, with her back to the device. "You will see," Neir-let's voice whispered.

Suzanne continued to concentrate, sometimes in the evenings, sometimes in the early mornings before the others were awake. Her days consisted of long periods in front of the device, punctuated only by the need to return to the dome for sleep and, less often, food.

Gabe came to her once, as she sat by the highway. He carried her and her device back to the dome and insisted upon forcing food down her throat. He hid the device in his room, saying he would give it back "when she looked healthier." Suzanne shrugged at this, by now indifferent to her bony limbs and slightly swollen belly. She wondered vaguely if she was pregnant; her period had not yet arrived. She spent several days lying on her mat, passively bearing Gabe's ministrations and wondering what Joel's child would be like. But after a week, her womb bled once more and she knew that there was now nothing left of Joel except the decaying body under a mound.

She regained her strength and managed to steal her device from Gabe's room while he slept. She fled from her dome and resumed her vigil farther up the highway. She ate her meals in another dome and slept in its large main room, arms draped over the metal object.

She often began her meditations while a group of Aadae sat in the road greeting the dawn. Her mind became clearer, more conscious of the things around her. She focused on a series of sharp images: the shadows of the seated, swaying Aadae, slender and elongated, rippling along the bumps and crevices of the pavement—

the blinded eyes of the robed aliens, violet irises afloat on a sea of white, with pupils that became small dark tunnels into darkness—

a strand of blue-black hair on a golden cheek, caressed by the invisible fingers of a breeze, becoming a long moustache over a lip—

a blade of grass among its fellows, its roots deep in the ground, attempting to draw moisture from the dandelion that hovered over it menacingly.

Her mind uncoiled and floated above her, drifting over the seated Aadae. The domes beneath her grew smaller, becoming overturned bowls on a table and then the tops of mushrooms. She was soaring over the burned bones of the city, strewn in a black pit, an omen to be read by a giant seer. She felt no fear as her mind traveled over the Earth and did not attempt to draw it back. She circled over the city. The highways were asphalt runes, incomplete, leading only to the pit.

Her mind came closer to the ground and returned to her,

rushing through the domes where people still slept, dolls thrown on the mats by a careless child. She was staring once again at the metal apparatus in front of her.

Almost ready. It was a whisper, in her mind but not of it. The Aadae rose and began to walk back to their dome, leading their blinded sisters by the hand. Suzanne blinked. There were black spots before her eyes and she realized that she must have been staring at the sun for part of the time.

Her body was a burden which she hoisted to its feet. She would rest, and feed herself, then let her mind roam again.

An Aada near her began to wail. Suzanne opened her mouth and sang with her; her soprano was a bird flying over, then alighting on, the alien's clear mellow contralto. She soared effortlessly, and her crystalline tones circled over the lower voice, then flew on over the clouds to the sun.

Suzanne sat by the highway, away from the late afternoon shadows cast on the ground by the domes. She set her device in front of her and prepared her mind for its work.

She was suddenly frightened, and remembered the morning, long ago, when she had fled from the Aadae in fear. *Throw it away.* She recoiled from the metal construct before her. *Someone, please, tell me what to do.* The world was silent, the road empty.

Once more. She watched the blue stone on the device. It began to grow larger, drawing her mind into a blue vortex. She swam in a shimmering dark sea and shafts of light, sharp as spears of glass, pierced her eyes.

She was hurtling over the Earth, following the sun to the west. She moved through the eye of a storm and danced on the pinwheel of clouds. The Earth shrank beneath her and she turned to the moon, brushing against its rocky lifeless surface. Its craters were empty, its mountain peaks sharp, its shadows

cold. She fled from the moon and was lost in darkness, heavy
black velvet draped over her, pressing at her.

She pushed the blackness away. Now she was falling, spiral-
ing uncontrollably toward the sun. Its flaming surface was a
battleground screaming across space, crying for death, reaching out to immolate her. Two flares erupted on the surface
and became wispy appendages, the arms of a lover seeking an
embrace. *No.* The star thundered at her. Another flare rose
and flung her into the emptiness.

A whisper reached her, almost as insubstantial as the flare
dissolving around her. *Not yet, you are not ready.* Frightened,
she flew from the conflagration, moving outward until the
planets were round pebbles and the sun only a distant lantern.

An invisible web surrounded her, pulling her toward a far
red ruby glittering among diamonds. She passed a young
world, still boiling, streaked with red and yellow streams. The
red star in front of her grew larger and she drifted through its
diffuse strands, to be met on the other side by a shaft of blue-
white light. A tiny white sun circled the red star, a fierce
sentry ready to defend its tired companion. She was pulled on,
past a large gaseous world where heavy tentacled beasts fought
in green seas, past a blue star around which dead rocks re-
volved, past a yellow sun linking flare-arms with its twin. She
struggled against the web around her. *Take me back.* The web
traveled more rapidly and she could catch only a glimpse of
the worlds she passed.

Ahead of her lay clusters of suns, crowded together in the
galactic hub, revolving slowly with companions or shrieking in
death, murdering servant worlds around them. She whirled
over them and retreated into memory:

Herds of automobiles stampeded through the streets. Their
motors were an omnipresent growl, a subliminal threat.
Trucks, oblivious to the smaller beasts around them, rolled by

majestically; smaller cars made up for their lack in size by the use of clever tactics and, occasionally, increased belligerence. Suzanne walked the streets on a summer evening, clinging to Joel. She gazed up at his face and his eyes were momentarily two suns winking at her. She jostled a red-nosed drunk, rubbed elbows fleetingly with a young blonde woman whose cold green eyes became a green gas giant surrounded by rings. Ahead, a well-dressed silver-haired man shimmered, brushing aside luminous wisps before disappearing into a bar. Two adolescent girls flirted with three muscular boys dressed in embroidered denim jackets twinkling with constellations. She sniffed at the summer air: acrid odor of sweat, exhaust fumes, a whiff of after-shave, a charcoal-broiled steak, sulfur, ammonia, dust. Voices shrieked, babbled, murmured, roared, giggled, and bellowed, underscored by the insistent rumbling of the vehicles around them. She and the others began to retreat from the sidewalks, yielding them to the night. From her window, she could see the lighted windows in the towers around her. A dog was baying below. She heard a thunderous roar, then saw light on the street beneath her. Men on motorcycles screamed by, night creatures in search of prey.

A comet streaked past, throwing her from the starry city. She whirled through the tendrils of a nebula, spinning aimlessly into space. The intangible web which had held her disappeared. She was alone. She had no tears to cry for Joel, for her lost city, for the Earth now impossibly distant from her. She spun through the darkness, away from the pinwheels and discs of galaxies.

Something nearby was tugging at her mind. She drifted toward it, unable to resist. She did not belong here with her small fearful mind and her passive ineptitude. She could not deal with anything out here; she could not understand the processes that produced this immense spectacle, nor could she deal with it emotionally except as a series of frightening visions. Her mind seemed to contract, pushing in upon itself. *You are less than nothing here.*

Stellar corpses. She could not see them, but she felt their presence. Heavy chains dragged at her, drawing her on. She was a prisoner and assented to her bonds passively. It seemed somehow right that she should remain here, punished for having ventured too far.

Ahead, she saw a circle of blackness, darker even than the space around her, a deep well blotting out the nearer galaxies.

She was falling, tumbling forward into an endless pit. The black well grew wider. She cried out soundlessly and tried to crawl away with nonexistent limbs. *But I should wake up now.* The well surrounded her and she continued to fall.

The web was around her once more. *Pull away.* She tried to grasp the mind near her. The black pit was luring her on, teasing her with strands of light, whispering promises. *Resist.* The other mind touched her and she clung to it, struggling away from the hole in space.

Help me, she called to the other.

Help yourself. She pushed and the hole became a distant blot, then faded from sight. Streaks of blue and red light raced past her and she was ripped into a thousand pieces, beads on the thread of time. A thousand cries echoed in the vault of space and became one scream.

She was in the web, hovering over the Earth. She flew closer and rested above a pink cloud over her domed settlement. It was already morning below and she could see tiny specks huddled together on the highway.

You will grow stronger, the other mind whispered to her. *You will travel with the other minds of space, streaking among the stars with tachyonic beings who have transformed their physical shapes ages ago. You will meet those who abandoned their bodies but lurk near their worlds, afraid to venture further. And if you are very strong, you may approach a star where the strongest dwell, ready to fight you if you intrude. They will try to fling you far away, but if you contend with them long enough, they will reveal their secrets and allow you to join them. Your mind will grow stronger with each journey, and when your body can no longer hold it, you will leave it behind, a garment which you have outgrown, and journey among the stars. You will learn all one can learn here and then move on to where there is only unending reflection. Do you understand?*

Yes. She was sitting by the highway once again, held by the receptacle of her body. Neir-let was with her, clasping her hand.

"There is one more thing to do," the Aada murmured. "Are you strong enough, or must you rest?"

"Now," said Suzanne. Her mind floated up, brushed against Neir-let's, then leapt from her across the Earth. She was a spark, a burst of lightning striking every human brain she found, leaping from one to the next. She seized a group of minds and flung them away, watching them leap to other minds. Then she gathered them all to her and wove them into her net, four billion strands, and flung them from the Earth. They cried out to her, some in fear, others in awe, still others in delight. She drew them back and wound the fabric around her, caressing each thread.

She was once more at Neir-let's side. Exhausted, she rested her head on the Aada's shoulder. Neir-let's hand brushed her hair gently. Trapped in her body, Suzanne could still feel the bonds that linked her mind with all of humanity, and knew that they were now linked for all time. They would never be alone again, isolated and apart, shadows lingering in separate caves. However distant they might be, in thought or space, whatever they might do by themselves, they would all be joined as closely as lovers.

Neir-let stood up and removed the blue stone from the metal device. "You no longer need this," she said, gesturing at the apparatus. The Aada pulled a pointed knife from the belt over her briefs, reached over and pricked Suzanne's forehead, then pressed the stone against it. Suzanne bore the slight pain silently, wincing a bit, becoming calm as the stone pulsed between her temples. "This will help you to focus your mind, but soon you will not need it either."

Suzanne lifted her hand to her head, touching the stone. Other aliens nearby were already at work, embedding the small stones in the foreheads of people seated by the road. She stood up. A group of boys, stones glittering on their brows, approached her, palms open in thankfulness. She reached out to them with her mind and embraced them, crying out silently in joy.

Suzanne, clothed only in a tattered robe, stood in the doorway of a dome. The Aadae would teach humanity all that they knew before leaving for another world. Then mankind would have to ready its own ships and prepare to save another race from the oblivion of death. She knew her body would not last long enough to undertake the journey, but she would be with the ships, helping them to locate beings that still huddled together in fear.

She looked around her. The body of Gabe Cardozo was nearby, propped up against a wall, face empty of expression. Rivulets of saliva ran down his beard and she smiled, knowing that his mind was out among the stars. Other people sat in small groups with Aadae, trying to learn what was necessary for their future voyage.

She had done her share, and knew no more would be asked

of her. She left the dome and walked to the highway, wanting only to roam through space again. She joined the group of Aadae seated in the road, blind eyes staring upward. A naked child ran past her, heedless of the festering sores on his arms and belly.

She sat down next to the Aadae and lifted her eyes to the flaming disc overhead. Her mind floated up effortlessly, drifting through the clouds.

The turbulent yellow star ahead seemed to beckon her. *I'll be ready for you, I'll take your wisdom with me before you fling me away.* She unfurled her wings and flew toward the sun.

In This Image

Alan Brennert

A truly alien being isn't likely to think as a human does; as we explore the reaches of interstellar space we're likely to come into contact with creatures whose ideas and attitudes will challenge our most deeply set emotions. How might we cope with these different views of the universe? (And how might those aliens cope with our own ideas?)

Alan Brennert is another alumnus of the Clarion workshops in science fiction writing; his stories have appeared in Analog, Infinity, *and* Vertex.

The ship limps into sensor field, a tired shell crawling along on sporadic bursts of fusion power—this is not its normal speed since Mind informs me that according to its configuration the alien could support twice the velocity it now has. I check my own speed and attempt contact, but there is no response.

I pull the ship from our set course and veer off toward the damaged vessel. I can see through Mind's eye that there is a jagged hole in the alien's propellant units; the fusion is emergency propulsion, possibly automatic. Detectors show the presence of debris lodged in the ship's generators—collision with matter, perhaps, although such a ship must have had meteor shields. How was the damage incurred?

I lay aside the question and concentrate on linking up with the alien's airlock. The design is not markedly dissimilar from my own, but sufficiently so to prevent hermetic sealing. There is linkage, but I cannot possibly cross over into the alien alive.

I must die first.

I put the ship under Mind control and leave the bridge, walking quickly through the narrow yellow hallways, yellow with the pulse of Mind's thoughts as Mind holds the ship in an electronic fist. I come to the airlock and, yes, there is sufficient difference in design between the two to allow leakage of atmospheres—between our ships is a vacuum. Perhaps it is for the best; there is no telling how the alien would react to the atmosphere of my ship. I stand before the lock and reach out to Mind.

—Ready.

I feel a sharp stab of power as Mind touches my thoughts, a white flash of light flames behind my eyes and fires to yellow, and then I die.

When I live again, I am in the alien's ship. The airlock has shut behind me. I look down at my hand: the golden glow is dying from my fifth and sixth fingers as Mind's control of my body leaks away. I look at a pocket chronometer; only a short time has passed since Mind shut my body functions down to minimal and took control of what was left, walking/floating me across the stinging vacuum of the airlock. I stare down at my chest—it still retains a yellowish tint as Mind holds my lungs in his grasp, adapting them to the odd atmosphere of this ship.

My mind is my own, now, and I look around the ship, searching for life. It is a small, cramped spacecraft, of alien but advanced design. It is obviously a scoutcraft of some sort, possibly not meant for more than one or two occupants. I walk through its dim, low-ceilinged passageways, looking for the pilot's cabin.

I find it; the door is jammed shut, its metal buckled into unyieldingness. I try to open it but my flesh is too weak for the task.

Or perhaps it is my mind that is too weak.

—Mind.

—Yes?

—My hand. Kill my hand.

—For how long?

—Long enough to break into this compartment.

—Ready.

My hand turns yellow with Mind's control, my hand turns dead at Mind's touch—and then it is bolting forward of its own accord, striking out at the tough metal before me, rearing back at the first dent, striking out again and again and again until the metal twists and buckles and the door rips open.

I watch, unfeeling, until it is done.

—Enough, Mind.

My hand stops.

—Acknowledged.

The glow fades just a little; not completely. There is still a yellow pallor to it . . . I can flex the fingers, but there is a numbness to them.

—Give me back my hand, Mind.

—Impossible. Tissue damage incurred during control. Relinquishment would result in severe pain, impairing rescue efficiency.

I look at my hand. It is bleeding, pale white blood as pale as my hand would be normally—it is only Mind's yellow grip that keeps me from feeling the pain that that blood brings.

—Mind: can you step down the flow of blood?

—Affirmative.

—Then do so, and give me increase in control in proportion to decrease of pain level.

Brief hesitation. Then:

—Done.

I can feel moderate control of my fingers seeping back into my flesh as the blood slows to a trickle. Somewhere there must be tremendous pain waiting to hurt, but I do not feel it. I proceed through the ragged hatch into the pilot's compartment.

Total destruction. Navigation panels apparently exploded and were torn from the deck, striking out at the walls of the ship and shredding the first layers of insulation. The cabin is still airtight, but just barely. Equipment is charred and melted. Seats are no longer seats but vaguely recognizable masses of molten steel. And beneath one fallen computer panel—

The alien; obviously not in its normal shape or form; obviously dying.

I go to its side and crouch there, trying to get a handhold on its body, but it is *flesh*, nothing more, nothing distinct . . . a thing made of mud and rain. There is no telling from what planet it came, to what race it belongs—but it is alive. As with the ship, just barely so.

I lift the fallen panel from its body with arms briefly strong and yellow, then try again to grab hold of the injured alien. Mind, too, grabs hold of it, and suddenly I am carrying what

might be soft, sculptured gold. I begin to walk back to the
hatch when Mind touches me:
   —Does the ship have a Mind?
I halt, look around me. Glass eyes staring blindly out from
crippled panels. Silent screaming metal.
   —No. Computers, rudimentary Minds.
   —Information salvageable?
   —I think not.
   —Then into what form must the alien be put?
I do not answer. There is no answer. I begin walking out
of the cabin again, and my eye lingers on every machine,
searching for some clue to the alien's form. I see nothing.

At the airlock I look for markings that might tell something
of the ship and its passenger. All that is emblazoned on the
door is a map of a planetary system in dull gray—a yellow star
at center, a bright blue disk third from the star, and nine
planets.

And then the airlock opens and I die once more.

By the time I return to the ship, Mind has analyzed the
atmospheric content of the alien's environment and has set
a life-support module accordingly. It is waiting for me when
I blink back into consciousness, and I carefully deposit the
alien flesh into it. The module, too, glows yellow with Mind;
as the alien is caught in the globe's nullgrav web, Mind lets
go of it. Control of my right hand is still denied me—a faint
gold to anesthetize the injury. Mind sends the module on
ahead of me to the infirmary; I follow.

Once inside the medical station I have Mind send us back
on course to homeworld; the piloting computers take over the
simple navigational tasks and Mind's glow leaves the ship. It
remains in module and hand. I make certain that the alien
will survive until I can tend to my limb: it can; Mind has

reproduced the atmosphere exactly, a nitrogen-oxygen mixture at a ratio of 78/21, with additional minor gases. I quickly minister to my wound.

When I have finished I ask Mind to withdraw. The glow vanishes and sharp needles of pain prick my flesh. I ignore them and go to the alien.

There is no *telling*.

—Mind: begin probe of alien's computers, such as remain.

—Probe completed during transfer.

—Good. Data of any value?

—Minimal. Some navigational information; alien's home-world pegged on our starcharts.

—Have we data on native life forms?

—No survey ever made.

Another world charted. I feel a minor thrill at the thought but suppress it.

—Can you reproduce gene pattern?

—Too complex for easy analysis. It would take time.

—Does the alien *have* time?

Mind hesitates as it runs a golden finger over the outworlder suspended in the life-module; then:

—No.

I look down at the alien as it breathes the air of the module, its flesh moving rhythmically, pulsing in the glass sphere like some great one-celled creature, mindless in its unconsciousness; alive but hurting. Without a guide, we cannot put it into its normal form through reconstruction; without a guide, it must either remain in the present condition . . . and die . . . or assume a form stored in our medical records.

But whatever form it is to take, it will have to live in this ship until it makes landfall. It will have to breathe this air, walk in this gravity, assimilate ship's tailored synthetics—and there is only one form suited to the ship's environment.

—Mind.

—Reading.

—Prepare the alien for molecular reconstruction. Scan its memory chain and duplicate in data banks until needed.

—What is to be the guide?

I look at the alien again. I feel a sudden weight bear down upon me.

—I am.

—The alien will live.

The alien will live. Why do Mind's thoughts feel sharp and irritating, like the pain now gone from my hand? There is no such edge to Mind's touch . . . it can only be apprehension on my part. I try to ignore my fears and settle attention on the alien.

Or is it alien still?

—Have you confirmed memory transfer?

—Affirmative. Full reflex correlation.

—Bring it awake, then.

The medical bed on which the alien lies glows a brief yellow. The fluid flowing intravenously into the alien's arm stops, reverses itself, and a new liquid pulses into the bloodstream, a red stimulant. Then the clear nutrient fluid comes in again and the yellow fades from the bed.

The alien stirs. It tries to open its eyes, then shakes its head in an attempt to shed sleep. Its lids open and I see its wide black eyes, moist and dull, roll upward in its head as it searches for a familiar sight.

Words emerge from its mouth—at least they must be words, some star-distant language. I put my hand on its arm and it sees me for the first time; it recoils a bit, then calms. It has not yet looked at itself.

"Speak my tongue," I say to it. "You know how, we taught

you. While you dreamed. You understand what I am saying, do you not?"

Its eyes remain wide with shock for several moments, and then it nods. "I . . . yes, I . . . can. Oh my—"

The word is lost to me. I hold its arm tighter and feel a tenseness. "Look at yourself," I tell it. "*Look* at yourself."

It lowers its gaze and stares at its body. It emits a short, shocked sound, and then it curls the lower part of its mouth, expecting to find something there. But this obviously does not concern the alien very much; it is staring at the rest of its body.

It sits up, at first with deliberate slowness, then quickly as it panics; it takes its hand and feels its chest, feeling the pale smoothness. And then it sees what it is touching itself with and draws away its hands, its eyes flicking from finger to finger as if counting.

It looks at its thin white legs and feels each of their three joints. It does the same with its arms. It looks at its black eyes in the pale blue reflective surface of a nearby wall: it rolls those eyes around in their sockets, perhaps searching for color other than blackness. It looks at its thin mouth, its flat aural orifices, its smooth forehead . . . and it touches a spot between the eyes and above the mouth where it seems to feel something should belong.

And then it looks at me.

"How . . . ?" it says, and the word is strained, uncomprehending. "Why . . . ?"

"Your ship," I tell it, "was destroyed. Collision of some sort. You'd know better than I."

It nods dully. "Yes . . . collision. Contraterrene . . . destroyed generators. Power feedback and the bridge died around me . . ."

"You were injured. Dying. We—I—brought you here. You . . . *did* want to be kept alive?"

For a moment it hesitates. "Yes," it says at last, but it sounds uncertain.

"Your data stores were wiped out. We had no way to tell your form short of genetic analysis, and there was no time for that; you were . . . shapeless. There was only one form that seemed practical."

It does not reply. It is touching its face.

Finally it asks, "Who are you?"

"Paol. I am a star mapper, a world charter. This is my ship."

"Mav Durham. I am . . ."

It stops suddenly, as if remembering what it was.

"I am a . . ."

A look of fear grips its face as it struggles to feel something. It shuts its eyes.

"I *was* . . ."

And its hands move down to its groin, feeling, searching, moving slowly—fearfully—over the junction, over the smooth, seamless flesh that connects trunk and thigh, and its fingers begin to shake as it does . . .

"I had . . . I *had* a . . ."

It breaks off into sobs, leans back onto the bed, which glows yellow as Mind injects the alien with sedative. It lies there quietly until it lapses into sleep. But I think I hear what it is trying to say, the loss it weeps for, and I wish I could share its sorrow.

I had a sex.

But the words are so very alien. So very odd.

After a day of rest, the alien has left Medical and seems content as it explores the ship. In asking me whether it was allowed to do so, it spoke curtly, with little inflection, as if trying to hold back either sorrow or anger. I allowed it free run of the ship and now it has come to the bridge.

It stands gazing out the wall-sized screenports at the stars. I think it has ceased to search for familiar patterns in them; already we are parsecs distant from the hulk of its old ship. The way the alien stares at the blackness disturbs me, however; it is a search for a home long gone, a longing and an ache. I am uncomfortable around this alien, this Mav Durham.

It turns from the screens, looks around itself at the brightly blue instruments that line the bridge, and then looks at me. "How soon before you make homefall?"

"A few weeks," I say. "You're fortunate that I found you on my return trip. Once we reach homeworld I'm sure that the stellar authorities will take you to your own system. They have ships equipped for hole jumps that mine cannot make."

The alien nods absently. It moves over to a navigational bank, a smooth piece of reflective plasteel. For a moment it eyes its image in the metal, then casts its gaze downward a little. "I . . . am grateful," it says suddenly, and I turn to look at it. "I don't think I would have liked to die out there," it adds softly.

"What difference if you had died on takeoff, on your home planet?"

It makes an odd movement of its shoulders. "Very little, I suppose, but . . . well, someone would know, that's all. Out here, death is a lonely thing."

I nod. "Out here, life is a lonely thing."

It smiles sadly. "Yes, but there was always the knowledge that when you return . . . when you get back . . . it's all over, that loneliness. Not now."

"Why is that?"

It stares at me. "What do you mean, why? Because I'm no longer a part of the world I left. I'll be an alien to my own people. You can't reconstruct me again; you said my molecular structure couldn't take the strain. This is my mask and I wear it for all time: I'll never belong to my race again."

"Belonging is important to you."

"It's not to you?"

"In different ways. You feel the need to belong to something greater than yourself—a race, a world. Only natural. But you miss your world for that reason. I miss mine because it is beautiful, not because it is mine. There are other beauties I can miss as much."

"Then what *do* you belong to?" it asks.

I hesitate. "Some of us belong to each other. Two wholes, three wholes, four wholes, combined to make a greater wholeness. But we are still individuals and would not relinquish that for the sake of being a *part*."

"A wholeness?" It seems to turn the word over in its mind. "Mental or physical?"

"Both."

It looks at me and I see a faint stirring of—what?—that which I feel when I sight a familiar star—in its eyes. "I thought you had no organs of reproduction. I certainly don't."

"We reproduce ectogenetically, though I fail to see the connection between that and wholeness. It has been a mechanical process for centuries before I was born."

"But . . ." It struggles to comprehend simplicity. "If something were to happen to your culture . . . war, or barbarism . . . your race would die out."

"Then it would deserve to."

It nods slowly. "I see." But it is not really interested in this. "The wholeness, though, the need—"

"Need? How can need be involved with wholeness?"

"But you . . . you need the other wholes to make a larger whole. Don't you?"

I shake my head. "A wholeness is always welcome, but it will not come unless all parties work for it. What comes is to be accepted. What does not should not be mourned."

"Passive acceptance of your environment?" The words are edged in cold.

"Not at all." I am beginning to find this irritating. "After working for whatever we desire, we may be content in knowing that we *have* worked for it, and the outcome must be accepted so that one can go on to other things. A wholeness is to be desired, but one must be whole without the greater being. Need implies an emptiness."

"And when you miss the beauty of your world . . . is that not an emptiness?"

I hesitate again. "No. Not fully. There are other ways to fill the emptiness: space, and stars, and Mind."

It walks away from the navigation bank, moves over to the starcharts that are frozen onto the screens to my left. "Have you a wholeness with Mind?"

"After a fashion."

"Mentally?"

"Of course."

"And physical wholeness—"

"—initiated by spiritual wholeness. The mind sharpens the bodily sensitivity . . . in all areas of the flesh."

"So you do have sex," it says, triumphantly.

"Again that word. We have physical pleasure, if that is what you call such pleasure on your world. But we do not *need* it." Annoyed at its insistence upon ascribing to me its own alienness, I add, "*You* do not need it."

And then I am sorry for that, for Mav Durham turns and does not speak for a long while as it stares out at the sky beyond the horizon of the ship.

"I still need," it says at last. "I need Earth. I need my people." It turns and glares at me. "For the first time in my life . . . I am glad for an emptiness, Paol. I am glad for it."

And then it turns and flees the bridge.

MEMO

FROM: SpCpl Mav Durham, Somewhere in Space
TO: Lee Kellogg, New Orleans, Louisiana, North American Conti-
nent, Planet: Earth, Star System Sol, Milky Way Galaxy, the
Universe
SUBJECT: The More Things Change

Lee:
Hadn't expected to hear from me so soon, had you? Well, postal
service isn't as bad as outworlders make it out to be. Everything
to please the tourists, you know—but that's neither here nor there.
(Come to think of it, I'm neither here nor there. Every time I
come up with a "here" for my jangled sensibilities to latch onto,
damned if it doesn't go and whip around like a Janus-bastard and
turn into a *there.*)

But I'm not writing you to bitch about my problems. How are
you, darling? Everything cozy on Terra? How's your brother?
Your parents? Good. Good.

Enough chitchat, then. *Now* to bitch about my problems.

The problem, my love, seems to be purely physical, and one
which I'm sure we as reasonable, liberated human beings—well,
adults, anyway—will not allow to be a barrier to our relationship.
As Paol is fond of saying, "Wholeness is made of diversity," and
if you knew Paol you'd want to shove that up his and/or her ass
as much as I do. (Of course, the question of whether Paol actually
has an ass in the terrestrial sense of the word has never come up,
but the alternative conclusion is that Paol is QED full of *something*. Well, maybe so. At any rate, I did not write this letter to
discuss alien physiology, or at any rate not Paol's.)

My problem, as I was saying, is a relatively minor one. I seem
to have lost my sex. To say nothing of my nose, my lips, one
kidney, and various other internal organs, although frankly it's not
the internal ones that are worrying me.

Oh yes: I have three-jointed arms. Marvelous for tennis. *First-
rate, Reggie! Love!*

That's another thing I seem to have lost somewhere. Love.

I'd enclose a holograph if I could, darling, but the local tourist bureau is horribly understocked when it comes to frills. Instead I will try to describe myself more fully, in the hopes that you will feel closer to me by my so doing:

I stand 2.4 meters tall, great for basketball but as I hinted above sports are not in abundance out here. No matter. My skin is white as chalk, my eyes are disks of polished obsidian, black and wide: no whites, all pupil. My vision encompasses a very wide spectrum now; no doubt they immerse the sperm and ova in carrot juice before spinning the little bastards together. (Don't ask!) My body is hairless and practically odorless. I have no olfactory membranes on my face, but my mouth performs some of that function. I am a tall, robust-looking specimen.

But you see, everything below the waist is more or less missing. It's somewhat like being a eunuch locked into a chastity belt. I'm even beginning to forget what was down there in the first place, rod or cunt or ceilingwax, and seeing Paol every day offers no illuminations. We're two of a kind, you see. I was reconstructed from Paol's molecular pattern, but Mind—now there you go again, asking questions; *trust* me, darling!—Mind was kind enough to provide me with my own memories. Wasn't that *considerate?*

Well, anyway, Paol. Paol is pretty much the same as I am, physically; the difference comes in in the old psychology. Has all these weird, really *alien* ideas about union and joining and need and all those kind of Universal Emotions. Doesn't think creatures should need: just desire and accept. If you didn't get that trihover that daddy promised you for Christmas, well, the hell with it, nothing to be done so don't worry your little genes over it.

(Except there are no daddies. Or mommies. Or maybe even children, how the hell should I know? You expect me to provide you with a goddamn travel guide or something?)

Funny thing is, love . . . sometimes I almost think the son of a bitch is right.

What's that? Oh, the question of Paol's Posterior. If Paol is an exact duplicate of me, could I not solve the puzzling case of the Alien's Arse simply by looking at my *own* hindquarters and making the logical extrapolations therefrom?

Well, that's a good point. Really it is. But you see . . . y'see . . .

I'm afraid to *look*, you see. I'm afraid to . . .

. . . *see* . . .

cc: Paol
    Mind
    God

—Paol, come awake.

I stir from my half-sleep, sit up on my bed. The cabin is very still and small around me and I feel, with an acuity born of dreaming, that there is something wrong in the way that Mind has addressed me.

Of course. *Paol, come awake.*

—Mind, why did you address me by name?

—For the same reason you address me. To identify specific thoughts to a particular listener. If you did not preface your thoughts with my name, it would be difficult to sort your musings from what you wish me to know.

—Yes, but the reverse is different. I cannot read all of your thinking, only that which you address to me; no name is necessary.

—Habit, then. You are not the only one to whom I address myself.

I shield my thoughts reflexively at this, hiding an irritation that I find scratching behind my awareness.

—You mean the alien?

—Yes.

—Does it . . . does it address you?

—Briefly. Curtly. It has not yet accepted my presence and regards me as an intruder. It speaks to me by voice, not mind.

My thought-shield drops, the scratching vanishes. But perhaps Mind has felt/heard it already.

—Why have you roused me?

—It is the alien.

The scratching.

—What about it?

—The materials you gave it to occupy itself . . . for writing, drawing . . . it formulated a missive with them.

—A missive? To whom, for life's sake?

—No one. Everyone. It was apostrophic in nature.

—How did you come by it?

—The alien dropped it in a waste chute, but I spotted the drop and initiated reclamation.

—We are always initiating reclamation. What did it say?

In answer my wall commscreen glows yellow and flicks into life. There appears there a series of lines and, I assume, words; as best I can judge, it was written in a shaky hand. But the lines are meaningless to me.

—Why would it write in its native language? It would only serve to confuse, two tongues vying for dominance in its mind.

—Perhaps it meant to keep the message private.

—Apostrophe usually is. Can you translate?

—Affirmative. I've made surface skims of the alien's memory and have a grasp of its tongue.

An unusual image. I lie back tiredly on the bed and watch the wallcomm. "On the screen, then."

The odd scribblings fade, the yellow Mindglow does not; and then the translated missive appears line by line before me. I follow each word as it appears, pausing only seconds over untranslatable words—I suspect their meaning from context. *Sex. Love.* The words are alien, but the problem is idiomatic; the undercurrent of emotion is familiar.

The last of the lines appear. I study the entire letter a few seconds, then turn away. The screen and the Mindglow fade.

—Mind, where is the alien?

—In its cabin. You're disturbed?

—It's not adjusting. By the time we reach homeworld, it is apt to be misanthropic. Withdrawn.

—So?

—You know as well as I that the alien will not—cannot—return to its world. Not as it is. It will have to make this land-fall its homefall; but if misanthropy continues to mount, it will never find a place there.

—Is it so very important, to have a place there?

I stare at the dark black floor at my feet a long moment before answering.

—It is important to have . . . a place.

I get up, look around my spare, sparse cabin, searching for Mind's glow in the spindly legged furniture burnished to mirror-blue. But Mind is invisible to me.

—How long to homefall, Mind?

—Eight days to orbital injection. Data store linkups for transferral of starmaps half-completed.

But I am not thinking of data transferral. I am thinking of clear aqua skies and mountains that lie proud and placid above warm lakes, of soft brown soil beneath my feet and between my fingers. And of the smell of the night.

I shed the memory and address Mind.

—I will speak to the alien. It must adjust.

—All things must adjust.

I break contact with Mind and leave my cabin, walk down the high twisting corridors to the deck below, where the alien is living. As I near its cabin I think of Mind's tone of thought, of those last words to me, and I wonder whether I should have asked more questions. But I cannot think of any to ask and it is too late as the cabin door slides open and I confront the alien.

I find it lying on its bed, looking disinterestedly at an entertainment tape.

"Mav Durham?"

It turns, and there is an ambivalence in its eyes: relief at monotony? annoyance at my presence?—I cannot place the conflicting emotions.

"Yes, Paol." Flat words. Tired.

"We will make landfall in eight days," I tell it. "You shall have to shuttle down to homeworld at that time and it might be wise of you to go through the culture tapes in order to . . . understand my world."

It looks at me. "Your world. Implication: the only world I have left?"

I nod impassively. "If you find you cannot return to your own, yes."

It looks at me with bitterness in its eyes. "I have no world. I'm caught between one that can exist only in memory, and one that I feel in my genes, but neither has a place for me. It's—" Its gaze softens, its voice grows calmer. "Goddamn it, it's important to have a place, Paol; it's all there is."

The echo rings in my head.

"Yes," I agree. "You must *make* a place for yourself, then. You say you cannot hope to have a life on your homeworld. Perhaps that is so. The only world remaining to you is . . . mine. You must adjust to it; you must forget your bitterness."

"And how could you tell the taste of bitterness?" it says sharply.

"I have learned. From you. Instead of trying to accept what you are, you have been trying to change everything around you to suit your past."

"Everything around me! I've had *nothing* to say about the world around me." Its voice is high and ragged with anger. "I woke to find myself in an alien body running toward an alien future. You played the role of a god, making me in your image!"

"And now, in kind, you seek to make *me* in *your* image.

You attribute to me emotions and philosophies that I have never known—love, sex, *need*. If you attempt this on home-world, you will be disappointed; the world will *not* change to suit you. You will well up with frustration and you will sour; and then you *will* have no place, Mav Durham."

It glares at me. "Congratulations, you've struck on a basic facet of human nature. Don't you see, Paol—no matter how hard I try to adjust to your homeworld, I'll be doomed to failure; my race has always tried to change its environment rather than itself. It's wrong, yes, but it's the way we are. How can I forget all that? How can I forget my world?"

"It can be done," I say.

"So easy to say! You make homefall in eight days. You Touch World, Paol; you have a *place*."

"Yes," I hear myself saying. "Here. My place is here." Why is my voice so soft? "I make no homefall, Mav Durham. There is never homefall."

It stares at me. I feel uncomfortable and suddenly wish to justify a position which needs no justification, explain a situa-tion that has long ago lost all explanation. "*This* is my world, this ship. It is a world not suited to many. One must . . . adjust. Acclimate. It can be done; you must believe that."

"No homefall?" Its voice is quieter, now. "I thought this was the end of your present tour of duty."

"It is. Each one lasts one decade."

Its mouth opens in shock. "A decade in space? How . . . how the hell do you stand it?"

"One . . . has to. One cannot survive so long in the empty spaces without . . . conditioning."

It hesitates. "What kind of conditioning?"

Why did I speak of it? "Psychological only. The alteration has not been duplicated in you."

"Psychological? In what way?"

I turn away from the alien, face a wall and seem to see the blacknesses that stretch beyond it. "They made me for space, but after a while I began to think the reverse; that space was made for me. The emptiness . . . like a cup filled with black silence. The stars waiting for a hand to come and mark them as real . . ."

The stars. The stars. "The joy of finding a new planet, the joy of discovery . . . and even if there were no new discoveries, even if all had been mapped . . . it would still be enough, for the shape of the sky keeps changing, a private infinity. It is . . ." I turn and face the alien again, lost for words to convey the beauty I have been made to love.

"A wholeness?" the alien says quietly.

I do not know. I make that odd shoulder movement which the alien uses to convey not-knowing. It averts its gaze.

"Eight days?" it says, not looking at me. "Eight days till homefall?"

"Yes."

It looks at me, then, with sadness in its eyes. "It has to be homefall, doesn't it?"

I nod.

The alien shuts its eyes, leans back on its bed and is silent. I back away and leave the cabin, thinking of what I have said, thinking of every word I have used to describe my life . . . and some that were left unspoken.

The beauty I have been made to love.

I was not made to love anything. I was made to *accept*. And yet . . .

Love feels right. So very horribly right.

In the engineering deck I make certain that all propulsion units are engaged for orbital injection in the next hour. I will have to take control from the automatic pilot and guide the ship into orbit myself; the maneuver is too complex for computer navigation. Mind could do it, but it is not necessary. I am completing check when I feel Mind at the periphery of my consciousness, but it is not Mind at full attention; more a whisper, a tap on the shoulder.

—Mind?

—I am linking you with my receptors. Listen.

—I have no time. Orbital insertion . . .

—Listen!

I do not argue; Mind's thoughts have a sharp edge of concern to them. I listen as I feel my awareness merge with Mind's, as I see/hear/feel through Mind's eye . . .

bridge: stars in background, winking blinking secret knowings against blackness: the empty spaces, the dark silences, and Mav Durham.

"Mind?" *A deep trouble, a deep hurt.*

—Reading.

"I don't doubt it. How soon to landfall?"

—Why not ask Paol?

"Because I'm asking you. How soon to landfall?"

—One hour to insertion.

Pain, a sharp aching. "How shall I be transported to the surface?"

—Singleshuttle. I will control it to a height of forty thousand; surface Minds will take over for the rest of the trip.

"I see." *But do not care. Help me, please—* "How long have you been traveling, Mind? You and Paol?"

—Fifty years this homefall.

"How much of Paol's life is that?"

—Approximately one-third.

"Then a third of my life is wasted on space, too. How much longer does he remain onship?"

—As long as he lives. Until he dies.

Horror, horror mixed with . . . "Are there others?"

—There are always others.

Black and bitter. "Yes. As long as space exists, there are others." *But why?*

—Perhaps it is unavoidable. Perhaps one either comes to live with the empty hours and the sunburst joys, or one . . . dies.

"Yes . . ." *What? How—* "How did you know I was asking why?"

—I could not help but know. Your entire being for that moment was Why. Your entire past was Why. All your future; all that was Why.

Resignation. "Another why, Mind. Why does the touch of your thoughts bring comfort but not peace?"

—You know that Why.

silence, eyes turned and staring at space, at the stars so many so lovely and one of them is Sol and Earth is lost; but to be here, to be a part of such beauty and immensity, to be part but still to be whole . . .

"I love it, Mind." *The sad beauty of knowing.* "You don't have to be conditioned to love it. To need it. Just live with it long enough to need its vastness, its wholeness . . . odd that I never knew that before . . . Paol."

Pain. "I didn't want to, perhaps. I didn't want to admit that I . . . that I could never go back to Earth, not even in human form. Rather than face that, I grew careless and a part of me ran toward that contraterrene. A part of me wanted death over this kind of life."

Help me. "I cannot make landfall, Mind. It would never be homefall. Not there, not on Earth. I have . . . a place."

—Here?

Sad slow yes.

—Fifty years or more, Mav Durham. You still have a pain and a need; I can feel it. You still have an emptiness as large as space. Fifty years of that?

Help me help me help
"God help me, yes." *And pause: and wait: and:*
—I cannot hear you, Mav Durham.
Hesitation, resignation, don't want to, I've got to, what's
left . . .
—God help me, yes, Mind. Yes. Yes. Yes.
help me—

And then I am wholly back in Engineering, Mind's eye is
lost to me, and I am alone.
I am alone.
I check my chronometer: forty-five minutes to insertion. I
must cut out the automatic and take control of the ship. I
take a hovershell to the bridge and as I skim along the decks
I try not to think of the cries I have just heard and felt. They
seem more than real to me; they seem doubly real, as if each
word echoed in some secret hollow of my mind.
But I am oddly relaxed, strangely at ease.
I leave the shallow cup of the hover and enter the bridge.
The alien is still there, eyes averted from the large brown
planet that hangs in the left screenport like a boulder on a
beach of black, private sand. Homeworld.
I move to the controls, do a routine check of the data
banks, and am about to switch off the computer pilot when I
hear the alien's voice behind me, cool and clear and easy.
"Paol."
"Yes?"
"Your world?"
"Yes. Once."
It nods. "How soon do you wish me to shuttle down?"
I feel a sharp biting shock and I do not know what to say,
what to do. "You—you are leaving?"
"Of course. What else is there for me?"
"But . . ." I am not supposed to know, not supposed to

have heard/felt/seen. Would it regard my listening as an intrusion? Yes. Yes. "I thought you might have—changed your mind. I am glad that you did not."

Am I?

"I'll head down to the shuttle bay and wait." It approaches me, outstretches a hand in what I take to be a gesture of farewell. I grasp its hand.

"Goodbye, Paol. Thank you."

I do not reply. There is something living in my fingers, something stirring in my flesh.

The alien turns and heads for the door.

But what made it change its mind, why has it turned from the spaces it loves, the world it cannot escape, the world *we* cannot escape . . .

Help me. Help me. Help

. . . me . . .

"Mav Durham." It stops, looks at me. "You do not want to go. I feel it."

"Do you?" It turns its back on me again and leaves the bridge. I follow, stand in the doorway as the alien walks down the corridor and the ship nears homeworld, oldworld, *damn*world.

"Mav Durham."

No reply.

"Mav Durham."

There is never any reply.

Help me. "Mav Durham, I need you."

It stops and turns and looks at me.

"I know," it says. "All parties must work."

It approaches me and for a moment I feel angry, and afraid. "Another change," I say, keeping distance. "You've altered me. Made part of me like part of you. For what?"

It looks at me still, the black of its eyes cut from space. "A wholeness," it says. "Accept, Paol." And there is part of me in its voice. I reach out to touch it, the ship calm yellow around us.

And for the first time in my life, I am glad for an emptiness. Glad for it.

What Friends Are For

John Brunner

With due respect to Robert Burns (and to God), it doesn't necessarily take the Supreme Being to give us the gift of seeing ourselves as others see us—as John Brunner shows in this amusing story of a robot from the stars who puts his alien viewpoint to work in a human household of the future.

John Brunner is the author of the Hugo-winning novel Stand on Zanzibar *and many other first-rate works of science fiction.*

After Tim killed and buried the neighbors' prize terrier the Pattersons took him to the best-reputed—and most expensive —counselor in the state: Dr. Hend.

They spent forty of the fifty minutes they had purchased snapping at each other in the waiting room outside his office, breaking off now and then when a scream or a smashing noise eluded the soundproofing, only to resume more fiercely a moment later.

Eventually Tim was borne out, howling, by a strong male nurse who seemed impervious to being kicked in the belly with all the force an eight-year-old can muster, and the Pattersons were bidden to take his place in Dr. Hend's presence. There was no sign of the chaos the boy had caused. The counselor was a specialist in such cases, and there were smooth procedures for eliminating incidental mess.

"Well, doctor?" Jack Patterson demanded.

Dr. Hend studied him thoughtfully for a long moment, then glanced at his wife, Lorna, reconfirming the assessment he had made when they arrived. On the male side: expensive clothing, bluff good looks, a carefully constructed image of success. On the female: the most being made of what had to begin with been a somewhat shallow prettiness, even more expensive clothes, plus ultrafashionable hair style, cosmetics, and perfume.

He said at last, "That son of yours is going to be in court very shortly. Even if he is only eight, chronologically."

"What?" Jack Patterson erupted. "But we came here to—"

"You came here," the doctor cut in, "to be told the truth. It was your privilege to opt for a condensed-development child. You did it after being informed of the implications. Now you must face up to your responsibilities."

"No, we came here for help!" Lorna burst out. Her husband favored her with a scowl: *Shut up!*

"You have seven minutes of my time left," Dr. Hend said wearily. "You can spend it wrangling or listening to me. Shall I proceed?"

The Pattersons exchanged sour looks, then both nodded.

"*Thank* you. I can see precisely one alternative to having your child placed in a public institution. You'll have to get him a Friend."

"What? And show the world we can't cope?" Jack Patterson rasped. "You must be out of your mind!"

Dr. Hend just gazed at him.

"They're—they're terribly expensive, aren't they?" Lorna whispered.

The counselor leaned back and set his fingertips together.

"As to being out of my mind . . . Well, I'm in good company. It's customary on every inhabited planet we know of to entrust the raising of the young to Friends programed by a consensus of opinion among other intelligent races. There was an ancient proverb about not seeing the forest for the trees; it is well established that the best possible advice regarding optimum exploitation of juvenile talent comes from those who can analyze the local society in absolute, rather than committed, terms. And the habit is growing commoner here. Many families, if they can afford to, acquire a Friend from choice, not necessity.

"As to expense—yes, Mrs. Patterson, you're right. Anything which has had to be shipped over interstellar distances can hardly be cheap. But consider: this dog belonging to your neighbors was a show champion with at least one best-of-breed certificate, quite apart from being the boon companion of their small daughter. I imagine the courts will award a substantial sum by way of damages . . . Incidentally, did Tim previously advance the excuse that he couldn't stand the noise it made when it barked?"

"Uh . . ." Jack Patterson licked his lips. "Yes, he did."

"I suspected it might have been rehearsed. It had that kind of flavor. As did his excuse for breaking the arm of the little

boy who was the best batter in your local junior ball team,
and the excuse for setting fire to the school's free-fall gymna-
sium, and so forth. You have to accept the fact, I'm afraid,
that thanks to his condensed-development therapy your son
is a total egocentric. The universe has never yet proved sufficiently intractable to progress him out of the emotional stage
most infants leave behind about the time they learn to walk.
Physically he is ahead of the average for his age. Emotionally,
he is concerned about nothing but his own gratification. He's
incapable of empathy, sympathy, worrying about the opinions
of others. He is a classic case of arrested personal development."

"But we've done everything we can to—"

"Yes, indeed you have. And it is not enough." Dr. Hend
allowed the comment to rankle for a few seconds, then resumed.

"We were talking about expense. Well, let me remind you
that it costs a lot of money to maintain Tim in the special
school you've been compelled to send him to because he
made life hell for his classmates at a regular school. The com-
panionship of a Friend is legally equivalent to a formal course
of schooling. Maybe you weren't aware of that."

"Sure!" Jack snapped. "But—oh, hell! I simply don't fancy
the idea of turning my son over to some ambulating alien
artifact!"

"I grant it may seem to you to be a radical step, but juvenile
maladjustment is one area where the old saw remains true,
about desperate diseases requiring desperate measures. And
have you considered the outcome if you don't adopt a radical
solution?"

It was clear from their glum faces that they had, but he
spelled it out for them nonetheless.

"By opting for a modified child, you rendered yourselves

liable for his maintenance and good behavior for a minimum period of twenty years, regardless of divorce or other legal interventions. If Tim is adjudged socially incorrigible, you will find yourselves obliged to support him indefinitely in a state institution. At present the annual cost of keeping one patient in such an establishment is thirty thousand dollars. Inflation at the current rate will double that by the twenty-year mark, and in view of the extensive alterations you insisted on having made in Tim's heredity I think it unlikely that any court would agree to discontinue your liability as early as twelve years from now. I put it to you that the acquisition of a Friend is your only sensible course of action—whatever you may think of the way alien intelligences have evaluated our society. Besides, you don't have to buy one. You can always rent."

He glanced at his desk clock. "I see your time is up. Good morning. My bill will be faxed to you this afternoon."

That night there was shouting from the living area of the Patterson house. Tim heard it, lying in bed with the door ajar, and grinned from ear to shell-like ear. He was an extremely beautiful child, with curly fair hair, perfectly proportioned features, ideally regular teeth, eyes blue and deep as mountain pools, a sprinkling of freckles as per specification to make him a trifle less angelic, a fraction more boylike, and —naturally—he was big for his age. That had been in the specification, too.

Moreover, his vocabulary was enormous compared to an unmodified kid's—as was his IQ, theoretically, though he had never cooperated on a test which might have proved the fact —and he fully understood what was being said.

"You and your goddamn vanity! Insisting on all those special features like wavy golden hair and baby-blue eyes and

—and, my God, *freckles!* And now the little devil is apt to drive us into bankruptcy! Have you *seen* what it costs to rent a Friend, even a cheap one from Procyon?"

"Oh, stop trying to lay all the blame on me, will you? They warned you that your demand for tallness and extra strength might be incompatible with the rest, and you took not a blind bit of notice—"

"But he's a boy, dammit, a *boy*, and if you hadn't wanted him to look more like a girl—"

"I did not, I did not! I wanted him to be *handsome* and you wanted to make him into some kind of crazy beefcake type, loaded down with useless muscles! Just because you never made the college gladiator squad he was condemned before birth to—"

"One more word about what I *didn't* do, and I'll smash your teeth down your ugly throat! How about talking about what I *have* done for a change? Youngest area manager in the corporation, tipped to be the youngest-ever vice-president . . . small thanks to you, of course. When I think where I might have gotten to by now if you hadn't been tied around my neck—"

Tim's grin grew so wide it was almost painful. He was becoming drowsy because that outburst in the counselor's office had expended a lot of energy, but there was one more thing he could do before he dropped off to sleep. He crept from his bed, went to the door on tiptoe, and carefully urinated through the gap onto the landing carpet outside. Then, chuckling, he scrambled back under the coverlet and a few minutes later was lost in colorful dreams.

The doorbell rang when his mother was in the bathroom and his father was calling on the lawyers to see whether the matter of the dog could be kept out of court after all.

At once Lorna yelled, "Tim, stay right where you are—I'll get it!"

But he was already heading for the door at a dead run. He liked being the first to greet a visitor. It was such fun to show himself stark naked and shock puritanical callers, or scream and yell about how Dad had beaten him mercilessly, showing off bruises collected by banging into furniture and blood trickling from cuts and scratches. But today an even more inspired idea came to him, and he made a rapid detour through the kitchen and raided the garbage pail as he passed.

He opened the door with his left hand and delivered a soggy mass of rotten fruit, vegetable peelings, and coffee grounds with his right, as hard as he could and at about face height for a grownup.

Approximately half a second later the whole loathsome mass splattered over him, part on his face so that his open mouth tasted the foulness of it, part on his chest so that it dropped inside his open shirt. And a reproachful voice said, "Tim! I'm your Friend! And that's no way to treat a friend, is it?"

Reflex had brought him to the point of screaming. His lungs were filling, his muscles were tensing, when he saw what had arrived on the threshold and his embryo yell turned into a simple gape of astonishment.

The Friend was humanoid, a few inches taller than himself and a great deal broader, possessed of two legs and two arms and a head with eyes and a mouth and a pair of ears . . . but it was covered all over in shaggy fur of a brilliant emerald green. Its sole decoration—apart from a trace of the multicolored garbage it had caught and heaved back at him, which still adhered to the palm of its left hand—was a belt around its waist bearing a label stamped in bright red letters —AUTHORIZED AUTONOMIC ARTIFACT (SELF-DELIVERING)—followed by the Patterson family's address.

"Invite me in," said the apparition. "You don't keep a friend standing on the doorstep, you know, and I am your Friend, as I just explained."

"Tim! *Tim!*" At a stumbling run, belting a robe around her, his mother appeared from the direction of the bathroom, a towel clumsily knotted over her newly washed hair. On seeing the nature of the visitor, she stopped dead.

"But the rental agency said not to expect you until—" She broke off. It was the first time in her life she had spoken to an alien biofact, although she had seen many both live and on tri-vee.

"We were able to include more than the anticipated quantity in the last shipment from Procyon," the Friend said. "There has been an advance in packaging methods. Permit me to identify myself." It marched past Tim and removed its belt, complete with label, and handed it to Lorna. "I trust you will find that I conform to your requirements."

"You stinking bastard! I won't have you fucking around in my home!" Tim shrieked. He had small conception of what the words he was using meant, except in a very abstract way, but he was sure of one thing: they always made his parents good and mad.

The Friend, not sparing him a glance, said, "Tim, you should have introduced me to your mother. Since you did not I am having to introduce myself. Do not compound your impoliteness by interrupting, because that makes an even worse impression."

"Get out!" Tim bellowed, and launched himself at the Friend in a flurry of kicking feet and clenched fists. At once he found himself suspended a foot off the floor with the waistband of his pants tight in a grip like a crane's.

To Lorna the Friend said, "All you're requested to do is thumbprint the acceptance box and fax the datum back to the rental company. That is, if you do agree to accept me."

She looked at it, and her son, for a long moment, and then firmly planted her thumb on the reverse of the label.

"Thank you. Now, Tim!" The Friend swiveled him around so that it could look directly at him. "I'm sorry to see how dirty you are. It's not the way one would wish to find a friend. I shall give you a bath and a change of clothes."

"I had a bath!" Tim howled, flailing arms and legs impotently.

Ignoring him, the Friend continued, "Mrs. Patterson, if you'll kindly show me where Tim's clothes are kept, I'll attend to the matter right away."

A slow smile spread over Lorna's face. "You know something?" she said to the air. "I guess that counselor was on the right track after all. Come this way—uh . . . Say! What do we call you?"

"It's customary to have the young person I'm assigned to select a name for me."

"If I know Tim," Lorna said, "he'll pick on something so filthy it can't be used in company!"

Tim stopped screaming for a moment. That was an idea which hadn't occurred to him.

"But," Lorna declared, "we'll avoid that, and just call you Buddy right from the start. Is that okay?"

"I shall memorize the datum at once. Come along, Tim!"

"Well, I guess it's good to find such prompt service these days," Jack Patterson muttered, looking at the green form of Buddy curled up by the door of Tim's bedroom. Howls, yells, and moans were pouring from the room, but during the past half-hour they had grown less loud, and sometimes intervals of two or three minutes interrupted the racket, as though exhaustion were overcoming the boy. "I still hate to think what the neighbors are going to say, though. It's about the most public admission of defeat that parents can make, to let their kid be seen with one of those things at his heels!"

"Stop thinking about what the neighbors will say and think about how I feel for once!" rapped his wife. "You had an easy day today—"

"The hell I did! Those damned lawyers—"

"You were sitting in a nice quiet office! If it hadn't been for Buddy, I'd have had more than even my usual kind of hell! I think Dr. Hend had a terrific idea. I'm impressed."

"Typical!" Jack grunted. "You can't cope with this, buy a machine; you can't cope with that, buy another machine . . . Now it turns out you can't even cope with your own son. *I'm* not impressed!"

"Why, you goddamn—"

"Look, I paid good money to make sure of having a kid who'd be bright and talented and a regular all-around guy, and I got one. But who's been looking after him? You have! You've screwed him up with your laziness and bad temper!"

"How much time do *you* waste on helping to raise him?" She confronted him, hands on hips and eyes aflame. "Every evening it's the same story, every weekend it's the same—'Get this kid off my neck because I'm worn out!'"

"Oh, shut up. It sounds as though he's finally dropped off. Want to wake him again and make things worse? I'm going to fix a drink. I need one."

He spun on his heel and headed downstairs. Fuming, Lorna followed him.

By the door of Tim's room, Buddy remained immobile except that one of his large green ears swiveled slightly and curled over at the tip.

At breakfast next day Lorna served hot cereal—to Buddy as well as Tim, because among the advantages of this model of Friend was the fact that it could eat anything its assigned family was eating.

Tim picked up his dish as soon as it was set before him and threw it with all his might at Buddy. The Friend caught it with such dexterity that hardly a drop splashed on the table.

"Thank you, Tim," it said, and ate the lot in a single slurping mouthful. "According to my instructions you like this kind of cereal, so giving it to me is a very generous act. Though you might have delivered the dish somewhat more gently."

Tim's semiangelic face crumpled like a mask made of wet paper. He drew a deep breath, and then flung himself forward across the table, aiming to knock everything off it onto the floor. Nothing could break—long and bitter experience had taught the Pattersons to buy only resilient plastic utensils—but spilling the milk, sugar, juice, and other items could have made a magnificent mess.

A hair's breadth away from the nearest object, the milk bottle, Tim found himself pinioned in a gentle but inflexible clutch.

"It appears that it is time to begin lessons for the day," Buddy said. "Excuse me, Mrs. Patterson. I shall take Tim into the backyard, where there is more space."

"To begin lessons?" Lorna echoed. "Well—uh . . . But he hasn't had any breakfast yet!"

"If you'll forgive my saying so, he has. He chose not to eat it. He is somewhat overweight, and one presumes that lunch will be served at the customary time. Between now and noon it is unlikely that malnutrition will claim him. Besides, this offers an admirable opportunity for a practical demonstration of the nature of mass, inertia, and friction."

With no further comment Buddy rose and, carrying Tim in effortless fashion, marched over to the door giving access to the yard.

"So how has that hideous green beast behaved today?" Jack demanded.

"Oh, it's fantastic! I'm starting to get the hang of what it's designed to do." Lorna leaned back in her easy chair with a smug expression.

"Yes?" Jack's face by contrast was sour. "Such as what?"

"Well, it puts up with everything Tim can do—and that's a tough job because he's pulling out all the stops he can think of—and interprets it in the most favorable way it can. It keeps insisting that it's Tim's Friend, so he's doing what a friend ought to do."

Jack blinked at her. "What the hell are you talking about?" he rasped.

"If you'd listen, you might find out!" she snapped back. "He threw his breakfast at Buddy, so Buddy ate it and said thank you. Then because he got hungry he climbed up and got at the candy jar, and Buddy took that and ate the lot and said thank you again, and . . . Oh, it's all part of a pattern, and very clever."

"Are you crazy? You let this monstrosity eat not only Tim's breakfast but all his candy, and you didn't try and stop it?"

"I don't think you read the instructions," Lorna said.

"Quit needling me, will you? Of course I read the instructions!"

"Then you know that if you interfere with what a Friend does, your contract is automatically void and you have to pay the balance of the rental in a lump sum!"

"And how is it interfering to give your own son some more breakfast in place of what the horrible thing took?"

"But Tim threw his dish at—"

"If you gave him a decent diet he'd—"

It continued. Above, on the landing outside Tim's door, Buddy kept his furry green ears cocked, soaking up every word.

"Tim!"

"Shut up, you fucking awful nuisance!"

"Tim, if you climb that tree past the first fork, you will be on a branch that's not strong enough to bear your weight. You will fall about nine feet to the ground, and the ground is hard because the weather this summer has been so dry."

"*Shut up!* All I want is to get away from you!"

Crack!

"What you are suffering from is a bruise, technically called a subcutaneous hemorrhage. That means a leak of blood under the skin. You also appear to have a slight rupture of the left Achilles tendon. That's this sinew here, which . . ."

"In view of your limited skill in swimming, it's not advisable to go more than five feet from the edge of this pool. Beyond that point the bottom dips very sharply."

"*Shut up!* I'm trying to get away from you, so—*glug!*"

"Insufficient oxygen is dissolved in water to support an air-breathing creature like a human. Fish, on the other hand, can utilize the oxygen dissolved in water, because they have gills and not lungs. Your ancestors . . ."

"Why, there's that little bastard Tim Patterson! And look at what he's got trailing behind him! Hey, Tim! Who said you had to live with this funny green teddy bear? Did you have to go have your head shrunk?"

Crowding around him, a dozen neighborhood kids, both sexes, various ages from nine to fourteen.

"Tim's head, as you can doubtless see, is of normal proportions. I am assigned to him as his Friend."

"Hah! Don't give us that shit! Who'd want to be a friend of Tim's? He busted my brother's arm and laughed about it!"

"He set fire to the gym at my school!"

"He killed my dog—he killed my Towser!"

"So I understand. Tim, you have the opportunity to say you were sorry, don't you?"

"Ah, he made that stinking row all the time, barking his silly head off—"

"You bastard! *You killed my dog!*"

"Buddy, help! *Help!*"

"As I said, Tim, you have an excellent opportunity to say how sorry you are . . . No, little girl: please put down that rock. It's extremely uncivil, and also dangerous, to throw things like that at people."

"*Shut up!*"

"Let's beat the hell out of him! Let him go whining back home and tell how all those terrible kids attacked him, and see how he likes his own medicine!"

"Kindly refrain from attempting to inflict injuries on my assigned charge."

"I told you to shut up, greenie!"

. . .

"I did caution you, as you'll recall. I did say that it was both uncivil and dangerous to throw rocks at people. I believe what I should do is inform your parents. Come, Tim."

"*No!*"

"Very well, as you wish. I shall release this juvenile to continue the aggression with rocks."

"*No!*"

"But, Tim, your two decisions are incompatible. Either you come with me to inform this child's parents of the fact that rocks were thrown at you, or I shall have to let go and a great many more rocks will probably be thrown—perhaps more than I can catch before they hit you."

. .

"I—uh . . . I—I'm sorry that I hurt your dog. It just made me so mad that he kept on barking and barking all the time, and never shut up!"

"But he didn't bark all the time! He got hurt—he cut his paw and he wanted help!"

"He did *so* bark all the time!"

"He did not! You just got mad because he did it that one time!"

"I—uh . . . Well, I guess maybe . . ."

"To be precise, there had been three complaints recorded about your dog's excessive noise. On each occasion you had gone out and left him alone for several hours."

"Right! Thank you, Buddy! *See?*"

"But you didn't have to kill him!"

"Correct, Tim. You did not. You could have become acquainted with him, and then looked after him when it was necessary to leave him by himself."

"Ah, who'd want to care for a dog like that shaggy brute?"

"Perhaps someone who never was allowed his own dog?"

. . . .

"Okay. *Okay!* Sure I wanted a dog, and they never let me have one! Kept saying I'd—I'd torture it or something! So I said fine, if that's how you think of me, let's go right ahead! You always like to be proven right!"

"Kind of quiet around here tonight," Jack Patterson said. "What's been going on?"

"You can thank Buddy," Lorna answered.

"Can I now? So what's he done that I can't do, this time?"

"Persuaded Tim to go to bed on time and without yelling his head off, that's what!"

"Don't feed me that line! 'Persuaded'! Cowed him, don't you mean?"

"All I can say is that tonight's the first time he's let Buddy sleep inside the room instead of on the landing by the door."

"You keep saying I didn't read the instructions—now it turns out *you* didn't read them! Friends don't sleep, not the way we do at any rate. They're supposed to be on watch twenty-four hours per day."

"Oh, stop it! The first peaceful evening we've had in heaven knows how long, and you're determined to ruin it!"

"I am not!"

"Then why the hell don't you keep quiet?"

Upstairs, beyond the door of Tim's room, which was as ever ajar, Buddy's ears remained alert with their tips curled over to make them acoustically ultrasensitive.

"Who—? Oh! I know *you!* You're Tim Patterson, aren't you? Well, what do you want?"

"I . . . I . . ."

"Tim wishes to know whether your son would care to play ball with him, madam."

"You have to be joking! I'm not going to let Teddy play with Tim after the way Tim broke his elbow with a baseball bat!"

"It did happen quite a long time ago, madam, and—"

"No! That's final! *No!*"

Slam!

"Well, thanks for trying, Buddy. It would have been kind of fun to . . . Ah, well!"

"That little girl is ill-advised to play so close to a road carrying fast traffic— Oh, dear. Tim, I shall need help in coping with this emergency. Kindly take off your belt and place it around her leg about *here* . . . That's correct. Now pull it tight. See how the flow of blood is reduced? You've put a tourniquet on the relevant pressure point, that's to say a spot where a large artery passes near the skin. If much blood were allowed to leak, it might be fatal. I note there is a pen in the pocket of her dress. Please write a letter T on her forehead, and add the exact time; you see, there's a clock over there. When she gets to the hospital the surgeon will know how long the blood supply to her leg has been cut off. It must not be restricted more than twenty minutes."

"Uh . . . Buddy, I can't write a T. And I can't tell the time either."

"How old did you say you were?"

"Well . . . Eight. And a half."

"Yes, Tim. I'm actually aware both of your age and of your incompetence. Give me the pen, please . . . There. Now go to the nearest house and ask someone to telephone for an ambulance. Unless the driver, who I see is backing up, has a phone right in his car."

"Yes, what do you want?" Jack Patterson stared at the couple who had arrived without warning on the doorstep.

"Mr. Patterson? I'm William Vickers, from up on the 1100 block, and this is my wife, Judy. We thought we ought to call around after what your boy, Tim, did today. Louise— that's our daughter—she's still in the hospital, of course, but . . . Well, they say she's going to make a quick recovery."

"What the hell is that about Tim?" From the living area Lorna emerged, glowering and reeking of gin. "Did you say Tim put your daughter in the hospital? Well, that finishes it! Jack Patterson, I'm damned if I'm going to waste any more of my life looking after your goddamn son! I am through with him and you both—d'you hear me? *Through!*"

"But you've got it all wrong," Vickers protested feebly. "Thanks to his quick thinking, and that Friend who goes with him everywhere, Louise got off amazingly lightly. Just some cuts, and a bit of blood lost—nothing serious. Nothing like as badly hurt as you'd expect a kid to be when a car had knocked her down."

Lorna's mouth stood half-open like that of a stranded fish. There was a pause; then Judy Vickers plucked at her husband's sleeve.

"Darling, I—uh—think we came at a bad moment. We ought to get on home. But . . . Well, you do understand how grateful we are, don't you?"

She turned away, and so, after a bewildered glance at both Jack and Lorna, did her husband.

"You stupid bitch!" Jack roared. "Why the hell did you have to jump to such an idiotic conclusion? Two people come around to say thanks to Tim for—for whatever the hell he did, and *you* have to assume the worst! Don't you have any respect for your son at all . . . or any love?"

"Of course I love him! I'm his mother! I do care about him!" Lorna was returning to the living area, crabwise because her head was turned to shout at Jack over her shoulder. "For you, though, he's nothing but a possession, a status symbol, a—"

"A correction, Mrs. Patterson," a firm voice said. She gasped and whirled. In the middle of the living area's largest rug was Buddy, his green fur making a hideous clash with the royal blue of the oblong he was standing on.

"Hey! What are you doing down here?" Jack exploded. "You're supposed to be up with Tim!"

"Tim is fast asleep and will remain so for the time being," the Friend said calmly. "Though I would suggest that you keep your voices quiet."

"Now look here! I'm not going to take orders from—"

"Mr. Patterson, there is no question of orders involved. I

simply wish to clarify a misconception on your wife's part. While she has accurately diagnosed your attitude toward your son—as she just stated, you have never regarded him as a person, but only as an attribute to bolster your own total image, which is that of the successful corporation executive— she is still under the misapprehension that she, quote un- quote, 'loves' Tim. It would be more accurate to say that she welcomes his intractability because it offers her the chance to vent her jealousy against you. She resents— No, Mrs. Patterson, I would not recommend the employment of physical violence. I am engineered to a far more rapid level of nervous response than human beings enjoy."

One arm upraised, with a heavy cut-crystal glass in it poised ready to throw, Lorna hesitated, then sighed and repented.

"Yeah, okay. I've seen you catch everything Tim's thrown at you . . . But you shut up, hear me?" With a return of her former rage. "It's no damned business of yours to criticize me! Nor Jack either!"

"Right!" Jack said. "I've never been so insulted in my life!"

"Perhaps it would have been salutary for you to be told some unpleasant truths long ago," Buddy said. "My assign- ment is to help actualize the potential which—I must remind you—you arranged to build into Tim's genetic endowment. He did not ask to be born the way he is. He did not ask to come into the world as the son of parents who were so vain they could not be content with a natural child, but demanded the latest luxury model. You have systematically wasted his talents. No child of eight years and six months with an IQ in the range 160–175 should be incapable of reading, writing, telling the time, counting, and so forth. This is the predica- ment you've wished on Tim."

"If you don't shut up I'll—"

"Mr. Patterson, I repeat my advice to keep your voice down."

"I'm not going to take advice or any other kind of nonsense from you, you green horror!"

"Nor am I!" Lorna shouted. "To be told I don't love my own son, and just use him as a stick to beat Jack with—"

"Right, *right!* And I'm not going to put up with being told I treat him as some kind of ornament, a . . . What did you call it?"

Prompt, Buddy said, "An attribute to bolster your image."

"That's it— Now just a second!" Jack strode toward the Friend. "You're mocking me, aren't you?"

"And me!" Lorna cried.

"Well, I've had enough! First thing tomorrow morning I call the rental company and tell them to take you away. I'm sick of having you run our lives as though we were morons unfit to look after ourselves, and above all I'm sick of my son being put in charge of— Tim! What the hell are you doing out of bed?"

"I did advise you to speak more quietly," Buddy murmured.

"Get back to your room at once!" Lorna stormed at the small tousle-haired figure descending the stairs in blue pajamas. Tears were streaming across his cheeks, glistening in the light of the living area's lamps.

"Didn't you hear your mother?" Jack bellowed. "Get back to bed this minute!"

But Tim kept on coming down, with stolid determined paces, and reached the floor level and walked straight toward Buddy and linked his thin pink fingers with Buddy's green furry ones. Only then did he speak.

"You're not going to send Buddy away! This is my friend!"

"Don't use that tone to your father! I'll do what the hell I like with that thing!"

"No, you won't." Tim's words were full of finality. "You aren't allowed to. I read the contract. It says you can't."

"What do you mean, you 'read the contract'?" Lorna rasped. "You can't read anything, you little fool!"

"As a matter of fact, he can," Buddy said mildly. "I taught him to read this afternoon."

"You—you what?"

"I taught him to read this afternoon. The skill was present in his mind but had been rendered artificially latent, a problem which I have now rectified. Apart from certain inconsistent sound-to-symbol relationships, Tim should be capable of reading literally anything in a couple of days."

"And I did so read the contract!" Tim declared. "So I know Buddy can be with me for ever and ever!"

"You exaggerate," Buddy murmured.

"Oh, sure I do! But ten full years is a long time." Tim tightened his grip on Buddy's hand. "So let's not have any more silly talk, hm? And no more shouting either, please. Buddy has explained why kids my age need plenty of sleep, and I guess I ought to go back to bed. Coming, Buddy?"

"Yes, of course. Good night, Mr. Patterson, Mrs. Patterson. Do please ponder my remarks. And Tim's too, because he knows you so much better than I do."

Turning toward the stairs, Buddy at his side, Tim glanced back with a grave face on which the tears by now had dried.

"Don't worry," he said. "I'm not going to be such a handful any more. I realize now you can't help how you behave."

"He's so goddamn patronizing!" Jack Patterson exploded next time he and Lorna were in Dr. Hend's office. As part of the out-of-court settlement of the dead-dog affair they were obliged to bring Tim here once a month. It was marginally cheaper than hiring the kind of legal computer capacity which might save the kid from being institutionalized.

"Yes, I can well imagine that he must be," Dr. Hend

sighed. "But, you see, a biofact like Buddy is designed to maximize the characteristics which leading anthropologists from Procyon, Regulus, Sigma Draconis, and elsewhere have diagnosed as being beneficial in human society but in dangerously short supply. Chief among these, of course, is empathy. Fellow-feeling, compassion, that kind of thing. And to encourage the development of it, one must start by inculcating patience. Which involves setting an example."

"Patience? There's nothing patient about Tim!" Lorna retorted. "Granted, he used to be self-willed and destructive and foul-mouthed, and that's over, but now he never gives us a moment's peace! All the time it's gimme this, gimme that, I want to make a boat, I want to build a model starship, I want glass so I can make a what's-it to watch ants breeding in . . . I want, I want! It's just as bad and maybe worse."

"Right!" Jack said morosely. "What Buddy's done is turn our son against us."

"On the contrary. It's turned him *for* you. However belatedly, he's now doing his best to live up to the ideals you envisaged in the first place. You wanted a child with a lively mind and a high IQ. You've got one." Dr. Hend's voice betrayed the fact that his temper was fraying. "He's back in a regular school, he's establishing a fine scholastic record, he's doing well at free-fall gymnastics and countless other subjects. Buddy has made him over into precisely the sort of son you originally ordered."

"No, I told you!" Jack barked. "He—he kind of looks down on us, and I can't stand it!"

"Mr. Patterson, if you stopped to think occasionally you might realize why that could not have been avoided."

"I say it could and should have been avoided!"

"It could not! To break Tim out of his isolation in the shortest possible time, to cure him of his inability to relate to other people's feelings, Buddy used the most practical means at hand. It taught Tim a sense of pity—a trick I often wish I could work, but I'm only human, myself. It wasn't Buddy's fault, any more than it was Tim's, that the first people the boy learned how to pity had to be you.

"So if you want him to switch over to respecting you, you'd better ask Buddy's advice. He'll explain how to go about it. After all, that's what Friends are for: to make us better at being human.

"Now you must excuse me, because I have other clients waiting. Good afternoon!"

The Author of the Acacia Seeds and Other Extracts from the *Journal of the Association of Therolinguistics*

Ursula K. Le Guin

One of the most important methods of communication between minds is art, but art is such a subjective thing that we might be overlooking many true works of artistic expression right here on Earth. Ursula Le Guin suggests that future researchers could discover a wide variety of art forms that exist around us even now, totally unsuspected. And she poses fascinating questions about the very nature of art.

Ursula K. Le Guin is one of the most highly regarded authors of modern science fiction, author of The Left Hand of Darkness, The Lathe of Heaven, *and many other classics of imagination.*

MS. FOUND IN AN ANT HILL

The messages were found written in touch-gland exudation on degerminated acacia seeds laid in rows at the end of a narrow, erratic tunnel leading off from one of the deeper levels of the colony. It was the orderly arrangement of the seeds that first drew the investigator's attention.

The messages are fragmentary, and the translation approximate and highly interpretative; but the text seems worthy of interest if only for its striking lack of resemblance to any other Ant texts known to us.

Seeds 1–13

[I will] not touch feelers. [I will] not stroke. [I will] spend on dry seeds [my] soul's sweetness. It may be found when [I am] dead. Touch this dry wood! [I] call! [I am] here!

Alternatively, this passage may be read:

[Do] not touch feelers. [Do] not stroke. Spend on dry seeds [your] soul's sweetness. [Others] may find it when [you are] dead. Touch this dry wood! Call: [I am] here!

No known dialect of Ant employs any verbal person except the third person singular and plural, and the first person plural. In this text, only the root forms of the verbs are used; so there is no way to decide whether the passage was intended to be an autobiography or a manifesto.

Seeds 14–22

Long are the tunnels. Longer is the untunneled. No tunnel reaches the end of the untunneled. The untunneled goes on farther than we can go in ten days [i.e., forever]. Praise!

The mark translated "Praise!" is half of the customary salutation "Praise the Queen!" or "Long live the Queen!" or "Huzza for the Queen!"—but the word/mark signifying "Queen" has been omitted.

Seeds 23–29

As the ant among foreign-enemy ants is killed, so the ant without ants dies, but being without ants is as sweet as honeydew.

An ant intruding in a colony not its own is usually killed. Isolated from other ants it invariably dies within a day or so. The difficulty in this passage is the word/mark "without ants," which we take to mean "alone"—a concept for which no word/mark exists in Ant.

Seeds 30–31

Eat the eggs! Up with the Queen!

There has already been considerable dispute over the interpretation of the phrase on Seed 31. It is an important question, since all the preceding seeds can be fully understood only in the light cast by this ultimate exhortation. Dr. Rosbone ingeniously argues that the author, a wingless neuter-female worker, yearns hopelessly to be a winged male, and to found a new colony, flying upward in the nuptial flight with a new Queen. Though the text certainly permits such a reading, our conviction is that nothing in the text *supports* it—least of all the text of the immediately preceding seed, No. 30: "Eat the eggs!" This reading, though shocking, is beyond disputation.

We venture to suggest that the confusion over Seed 31 may result from an ethnocentric interpretation of the word "up." To us, "up" is a "good" direction. Not so, or not necessarily so, to an ant. "Up" is where the food comes from, to be sure; but "down" is where security, peace, and home are to be found. "Up" is the scorching sun; the freezing night; no shelter in the beloved tunnels; exile; death. Therefore we suggest that this strange author, in the solitude of her lonely tunnel, sought with what means she had to express the ultimate blasphemy conceivable to an ant, and that the correct reading of Seeds 30–31, in human terms, is:

Eat the eggs! Down with the Queen!

The desiccated body of a small worker was found beside Seed 31 when the manuscript was discovered. The head had been severed from the thorax, probably by the jaws of a soldier of the colony. The seeds, carefully arranged in a pattern resembling a musical stave, had not been disturbed. (Ants of the soldier caste are illiterate; thus the soldier was presumably not interested in the collection of useless seeds from which the edible germ had been removed.) No living ants were left in the colony, which was destroyed in a war with a neighboring ant hill at some time subsequent to the death of the Author of the Acacia Seeds.

—G. D'Arbay, T. R. Bardol

Announcement of an Expedition

The extreme difficulty of reading Penguin has been very much lessened by the use of the underwater motion picture camera. On film it is at least possible to repeat, and to slow down, the fluid sequences of the script, to the point where, by constant repetition and patient study, many elements of this most elegant and lively literature may be grasped, though the nuances, and perhaps the essence, must forever elude us.

It was Professor Duby who, by pointing out the remote affiliation of the script with Low Graylag, made possible the first, tentative glossary of Penguin. The analogies with Dolphin which had been employed up to that time never proved very useful, and were often quite misleading.

Indeed it seemed strange that a script written almost entirely in wings, neck, and air should prove the key to the poetry of short-necked, flipper-winged water writers. But we should not have found it so strange if we had kept in mind the fact that penguins are, despite all evidence to the contrary, birds.

Because their script resembles Dolphin in *form*, we should never have assumed that it must resemble Dolphin in *content*. And indeed it does not. There is, of course, the same extraordinary wit and the flashes of crazy humor, the inventiveness, and the inimitable grace. In all the thousands of literatures of the Fish stock, only a few show any humor at all, and that usually of a rather simple, primitive sort; and the superb gracefulness of Shark or Tarpon is utterly different from the joyous vigor of all Cetacean scripts. The joy, the vigor, and the humor are all shared by Penguin authors; and, indeed, by many of the finer Seal *auteurs*. The temperature of the blood is a bond. But the construction of the brain, and of the womb, makes a barrier! Dolphins do not lay eggs. A world of difference lies in that simple fact.

Only when Professor Duby reminded us that penguins are birds, that they do not swim but *fly in water*, only then could the therolinguist begin to approach the sea literature of the penguin with understanding; only then could the miles of recordings already on film be restudied and, finally, appreciated.

But the difficulty of translation is still with us.

A satisfying degree of progress has already been made in Adélie. The difficulties of recording a group kinetic performance in a stormy ocean as thick as pea soup with plankton at a temperature of $31°$ F. are considerable; but the perseverance of the Ross Ice Barrier Literary Circle has been fully rewarded with such passages as "Under the Iceberg," from the *Autumn Song*—a passage now world famous in the rendition by Anna Serebryakova of the Leningrad Ballet. No verbal rendering can approach the felicity of Miss Serebryakova's version. For, quite simply, there is no way to reproduce in writing the all-important *multiplicity* of the original text, so beautifully rendered by the full chorus of the Leningrad Ballet company.

Indeed, what we call "translations" from the Adélie—or from any group kinetic text—are, to put it bluntly, mere notes —libretto without the opera. The ballet version is the true translation. Nothing in words can be complete.

I therefore suggest, though the suggestion may well be greeted with frowns of anger or with hoots of laughter, that *for the therolinguist*—as opposed to the artist and the amateur —the kinetic sea writings of Penguin are the *least* promising field of study, and, further, that Adélie, for all its charm and relative simplicity, is a less promising field of study than is Emperor.

Emperor! I anticipate my colleagues' response to this suggestion. Emperor! The most difficult, the most remote, of all the dialects of Penguin! The language of which Professor Duby himself remarked, "The literature of the emperor penguin is as forbidding, as inaccessible, as the frozen heart of Antarctica itself. Its beauties may be unearthly, but they are not for us."

Maybe. I do not underestimate the difficulties: not least of which is the imperial temperament, so much more reserved and aloof than that of any other penguin. But, paradoxically, it is just in this reserve that I place my hope. The emperor is not a solitary, but a social bird, and while on land for the breeding season dwells in colonies, as does the Adélie; but these colonies are very much smaller and very much quieter than those of the Adélie. The bonds between the members of an emperor colony are rather personal than social. The emperor is an individualist. Therefore I think it almost certain that the literature of the emperor will prove to be composed by single authors, instead of chorally; and therefore it will be translatable into human speech. It will be a kinetic literature, but how different from the spatially extensive, rapid, multiplex choruses of sea writing! Close analysis, and genuine transcription, will at last be possible.

What! say my critics—Should we pack up and go to Cape Crozier, to the dark, to the blizzards, to the —60° cold, in the mere hope of recording the problematic poetry of a few strange birds who sit there, in the midwinter dark, in the blizzards, in the —60° cold, on the eternal ice, with an egg on their feet?

And my reply is, Yes. For, like Professor Duby, my instinct tells me that the beauty of that poetry is as unearthly as anything we shall ever find on Earth.

To those of my colleagues in whom the spirit of scientific curiosity and aesthetic risk is strong, I say, imagine it: the ice, the scouring snow, the darkness, the ceaseless whine and scream of wind. In that black desolation a little band of poets crouches. They are starving; they will not eat for weeks. On the feet of each one, under the warm belly feathers, rests one large egg, thus preserved from the mortal touch of the ice. The poets cannot hear each other; they cannot see each other. They can only feel the other's *warmth*. That is their poetry, that is their art. Like all kinetic literatures, it is silent; unlike other kinetic literatures, it is all but immobile, ineffably subtle. The ruffling of a feather; the shifting of a wing; the touch, the slight, faint, warm touch of the one beside you. In unutterable, miserable, black solitude, the affirmation. In absence, presence. In death, life.

I have obtained a sizable grant from UNESCO and have stocked an expedition. There are still four places open. We leave for Antarctica on Thursday. If anyone wants to come along, welcome!

—D. Petri

Editorial—By the President of the Therolinguistics Association

What is Language?

This question, central to the science of therolinguistics, has been answered—heuristically—by the very existence of the science. Language is communication. That is the axiom on which all our theory and research rest, and from which all our discoveries derive; and the success of the discoveries testifies to the validity of the axiom. But to the related, yet not identical question, What is Art? we have not yet given a satisfactory answer.

Tolstoy, in the book whose title is that very question, answered it firmly and clearly: Art, too, is communication. This answer has, I believe, been accepted without examination or criticism by therolinguistics. For example: Why do therolinguists study only animals?

Why, because plants do not communicate.

Plants do not communicate; that is a fact. Therefore plants have no language; very well; that follows from our basic axiom. Therefore, also, plants have no art. But stay! That does *not* follow from the basic axiom, but only from the unexamined Tolstoyan corollary.

What if art is not communicative?

Or, what if some art is communicative, and some art is not?

Ourselves animals, active, predators, we look (naturally enough) for an active, predatory, communicative art; and when we find it, we recognize it. The development of this power of recognition and the skills of appreciation is a recent and glorious achievement.

But I submit that, for all the tremendous advances made by therolinguistics during the last decades, we are only at the beginning of our age of discovery. We must not become slaves to our own axioms. We have not yet lifted our eyes to the vaster horizons before us. We have not faced the almost terrifying challenge of the Plant.

If a noncommunicative, vegetative art exists, we must re-think the very elements of our science, and learn a whole new set of techniques.

For it is simply not possible to bring the critical and technical skills appropriate to the study of Weasel murder mysteries, or Batrachian erotica, or the tunnel sagas of the earthworm, to bear on the art of the redwood or the zucchini.

This is proved conclusively by the failure—a noble failure—of the efforts of Dr. Srivas, in Calcutta, using time-lapse photography, to produce a lexicon of Sunflower. His attempt was daring, but doomed to failure. For his approach was kinetic—a method appropriate to the *communicative* arts of the tortoise, the oyster, and the sloth. He saw the extreme slowness of the kinesis of plants, and only that, as the problem to be solved.

But the problem was far greater. The art he sought, if it exists, is a noncommunicative art—and probably a nonkinetic one. It is possible that Time, the essential element, matrix, and measure of all known animal art, does not enter into vegetable art at all. The plants may use the meter of eternity. We do not know.

We do not know. All we can guess is that the putative Art of the Plant is *entirely different* from the Art of the Animal. What it is, we cannot say; we have not yet discovered it. Yet I predict with some certainty that it exists, and that when it is found it will prove to be, not an action, but a reaction: not a communication, but a reception. It will be exactly the opposite of the art we know and recognize. It will be the first *passive* art known to us.

Can we in fact know it? Can we ever understand it?

It will be immensely difficult. That is clear. But we should not despair. Remember that so late as the midtwentieth century, most scientists, and many artists, did not believe that even Dolphin would ever be comprehensible to the human brain—or worth comprehending! Let another century pass, and we may seem equally laughable. "Do you realize," the phytolinguist will say to the aesthetic critic, "that they couldn't even read Eggplant?" And they will smile at our ignorance, as they pick up their rucksacks and hike on up to read the newly deciphered lyrics of the lichen on the north face of Pike's Peak.

And with them, or after them, may there not come that even bolder adventurer—the first geolinguist, who, ignoring the delicate, transient lyrics of the lichen, will read beneath it the still less communicative, still more passive, wholly atemporal, cold, volcanic poetry of the rocks: each one a word spoken, how long ago, by the earth itself, in the immense solitude, the immenser community, of space.